found a heart

D1607411

Emory Grey

Published by Emory Grey

Edited by Kiezha Ferrell at Librum Artis

Cover Design by Steamy Designs

Table of Contents

Author's Note

Potential Trigger Warnings: Female lead is a victim of revenge porn

If you are a victim of nonconsensual pornography ("NCP", also known as "revenge porn"), recorded sexual assault (RSA), or sextortion and you reside in the United States, please call the CCRI Crisis Helpline at 844-878-CCRI (2274)

Consent must come BEFORE any sexual activity of any kind. Consent must be active, voluntary, sober, and continuous.

Prologue

Kasie

My phone slips out of my hand and clatters to the floor, but the sound doesn't register. My eyes well up with tears, and my heart thunders in my chest as I slump to a seated position on the corner of my bed.

How could he?

Without warning, my vision begins to tunnel.

No, no, no.

"Daddy! It's happening again!" I yell and hear his footsteps fast approaching from the kitchen to my room.

"What's going on?" he asks, kneeling next to me.

"I can't breathe!" I cry out, trying

desperately to slow my breath down, but my stomach, arms, and feet are going numb, my heart is at the racetrack, and my mind is in worst-case-scenario mode. "I can't breathe, I'm going to pass out."

"Kasie, look at me," he says calmly, and I manage to follow his instructions, but just barely. "You're not going to pass out, you're just having another panic attack. It'll pass. But you do need to get ahold of your breath," he says as my numb hands begin to tremble. He leaves my room for a second and returns with a wet towel to press against my forehead. "Breathe deep with me, okay?"

"Okay," I say shakily as I drag breath into my tight chest, still battling the deadly what-if scenarios in my head. "Daddy, I'm scared."

"I know, sweet pea. I won't let anything happen to you. You're safe. Talk to me."

"About what?"

"Anything to get your mind off of what's happening right now. How'd the Lakers do last night?"

"They won," I say quickly, still fighting for my breath. "I really hate this."

"I know you do—"

"Why do I have to be like this?" I ask with a sob, tears trickling down my cheeks.

Two years ago, I was minding my own business, practicing driving with my dad, when we approached this long bridge that I had ridden over countless times before. I didn't know why at the time, but I always got nervous when I drove onto it. And there was this odd thought in my head—*what would happen if I jerked the wheel and drove off the side of the bridge?*

When I blinked it away, I had my first panic attack. It was absolutely terrifying, because I had no idea what it was or what brought it on; all I knew was that my body was going numb, I felt like I was having a heart attack, and I was sure I was suffocating.

When the anxiety and panic attacks didn't stop, I started going to therapy, and before long, I realized that, among other things, it was the fear of death that had the biggest grip on me, which made some sense because my mom died in a car wreck when I was eight years old.

I went through a phase where I didn't want

to leave home for anything. Not to swim, not to go on our monthly hike, not even to wristband night at the county fair. Eventually, my therapist helped me to understand my panic attacks and what I had to do to stay in control, but some are just harder to get a grip on than others. This is one of those.

I continue. "Every time I try to breathe, I feel like something steals my breath away. What happens if I can't pull myself out this time?"

"You've got this, you always do. You are strong, Kasie."

"I don't feel strong. I feel weak."

"Even strong people have weak moments. Now, let's get back on track. How many points did Kobe score?"

"Thirty-five. No, wait, thirty-eight. I forgot he hit a late three-pointer."

"Wow, so what does that make it? Three straight wins for the Lakers? I'm sad to say it, but I don't think my Bulls will make it to the playoffs this year."

"That's because they suck this year," I say, chuckling softly as I feel my breath slowing down but still in the fast lane.

"Well, I was just about to go get you an ice-cold water, but maybe I'll have you get up and walk with me to get it."

"Daddy," I whine and jut out my bottom lip.

He laughs and pats my knee as he stands up to go get the water for me.

When he returns with the water and hands it to me, he asks, "How are you feeling?"

I take a sip and breathe in the first deep breath since my panic attack started. "Better. Still a little shaky, but I think the worst is over."

Except, the worst really isn't over, because even though the panic attack is passing through, now I have to worry about the video that brought it on. A video that should never have been taken, let alone uploaded to Instagram for the world to see.

Two months later…

Everywhere I go, I feel like people look at me differently now. I can hear the whispers; I can feel the judgmental eyes burning into my skin. And I can't even count how many times I've waited on a table at the local café and asked if there was anything else I could get or do for them, and some stupid guy snickers and says, "how about a lap dance?"

Nothing will ever be the same for me again in this stupid small town. My dad says it'll pass, but he wasn't in the video handing lap dances out—I was. And he doesn't have to forget the humiliation. I do. And as long as I'm here, I have little faith in my ability to do that. People don't forget. So, the only way I can move on with my life and be free again, is to leave Rock Lake, South Carolina—to start over.

"I really don't like this idea," my dad says, holding the acceptance papers from San Diego State University.

I applied last month without him knowing, and because I've got insurance money from my mother's death in a trust, I didn't have to wrestle with the idea of committing some sort of fraud by signing financial aid paperwork for him. I feel bad for not telling him, but I'm certain he would find a way to convince me to stay and I just don't want to anymore.

"Do you just hate it because I'll be closer to the Lakers?" I ask, and he frowns. I giggle and grab one of the chocolate chip cookies that I just finished baking about ten minutes ago. "I'll be okay, Daddy. I've got a plan. I've done some research, and there's a few therapists I'm going to check out. I'm staying with Morgan in Del Mar, and she knows how to help if I need it, and I've even got a job interview at one of the restaurants a couple blocks away from the apartment."

Morgan is a good friend of mine who I kept in touch with after she moved away during our freshman year of high school.

He sighs heavily and takes a seat at our four-top dining table. "You know, protecting you has been the most important job I've held for the last eighteen years. I guess I always knew this moment was going to come, but I suppose I thought I'd be better prepared for it."

The sadness in his voice pulls at my heart, and this is why I waited to tell him, although it's not like it makes it any easier. I take a seat next to him, offering him a cookie like it'll make everything better. "I didn't mean to make you sad."

He accepts the cookie and then says, "You didn't make me sad, sweet pea. You've always made me proud. And you are your mother's daughter, because I can see it in your eyes, your mind is made up. I've always told you that you could do or be anything you want, so I won't stand in your way now. Hang tight one second; I have something for you, something I think your mother would want you to have." With that surprise, he takes a bite of his cookie and pushes out his chair.

I wait for him to return, and when he does, he's got the sparkly notebook that was her adventure journal. I remember the first time he showed it me, the week we discovered my fear of death. My mom, she kept this journal of all the crazy, adventurous things she did: pictures, inspirational quotes, her thoughts, even a picture of when I was born, because she was terrified that she wouldn't be a good mom, but she was. She was the best.

I smile softly and try not to let the tears sneak down my cheek as I start flipping through it again, but it's no use. "Am I making the right decision, Daddy?"

He smiles gently. "There is no growth in your comfort zone, and although I'd rather keep you here forever, I know I have to let you go. You are brave, just like your mother. You've got this, kiddo."

I swallow the knot in my throat and keep turning the pages of my mom's adventures until I get to one that speaks to me like it never has before. There's a picture of her skydiving taped on the inside and a quote beneath it.

I can't control when or how I die; I can only control how I live.

A rush of sweet and warm comfort surrounds me, and I breathe a confident sigh. "I want to live like her—free and fearless."

Chapter One

Kasie

Four years later…

Four years of combining therapy, meditation, and facing my fear of death one frightening, yet thrilling, activity at a time, and I can honestly admit that I've broken out of my shell. I'm living my best life.

My anxiety and panic attacks aren't gone. Sometimes, I can go months without having them, but eventually, something triggers me and they're back like a loyal friend. But, aside from the occasional slip-up, they don't paralyze me the way they used to. And for that, I am so damn proud of myself, because learning control when everything feels out of control is a gift.

I'm sitting at a sticky, circular bar table sipping on my third cranberry vodka in my favorite nightclub. Why is it my favorite? Because the bartenders don't believe in weak drinks, and the DJ always keeps the dance floor packed, which is great because dancing is my favorite. And tonight, I'm out celebrating me graduating from SDSU last week with my Bachelors in Business Administration— just one step closer to opening my own little bakery. Next is a rigorous, ten-month Baking and Pastry Certificate Program at the California Culinary Arts Institute. And with me to celebrate tonight is my best friend, Donnie, who, unlike me, needs a little more convincing to get out on the dance floor. And by convincing, I mean plenty of those strong drinks I mentioned. He's at the bar grabbing our next round right now, and hopefully he shows back up soon because I'm starting to taste more ice than cranberry. And the last thing I need is—

"Damn, girl, you look sexy as fuck in that little black dress," I hear a slurred voice from behind me say. "Your drink is looking a little dry. Tell you what, if you come dance with me, I'll buy you whatever you want."

Oh, how romantic.

I turn my head and smile politely at a guy who probably took forty-five minutes to get his hair so perfect. He's got a nice smile on his clean-shaven face, and I'm sure he's used to charming girls out of their panties with it, but I already know he's not my type. Not because of his looks but because of his mouth. Maybe it's the Southern girl in me, but I like a guy who talks to me like he's a gentleman.

"No, thank you."

"Ah, come on. Why not? You're too fine to be sitting here all alone."

"I'm actually waiting on someone."

"What's your name?" he asks, licking his lips and completely ignoring what I said.

"Kasie."

"I'm Brett. And might I say, you have the sexiest voice I've ever heard. Where are you from, Kasie?"

I roll my eyes internally. I swear, in my four years of living in Cali, I've met every single guy with a fetish for Southern accents. I don't even have a thick accent—it's soft, with just a slight drawl. I don't see what the big deal is, but apparently it makes them weak—their words, not mine. *And* I'm petite—5'1 and just over a hundred pounds to be exact—which seems to be some sort of icing on the cake.

"I'm from Del Mar. It's like twenty minutes away from here." I know he's really asking where my accent is from, but pushy guys don't get easy answers. He looks at me, perplexed, probably trying to figure out if my long, golden blonde hair is the reason I answered his question incorrectly.

"You're cute. Anyways, what do you say, just one dance until your friend shows up?" He leans in closer, and I wonder if I'm going to have to show him why my dad made me take jiu-jitsu classes growing up. "Do you see my buddies over there?" He points to a group of guys wearing big, drunk smirks. "They bet me I couldn't get you to dance with me. Are you really going to make a loser out of me?"

I rake my fingers through my hair and sigh. "Look, I'm sure you're a nice guy and all, but like I said, I'm waiting on someone—my boyfriend, to be exact. So, maybe you can find another girl to make you a winner tonight." Even after the boyfriend admission, he looks undeterred, but Donnie shows up just in time.

"Hey, baby!" I snap up from my chair and wrap my arms around Donnie's neck, almost making him spill the cranberry vodka and whiskey water he's carrying.

"Hey...*sweetheart*," Donnie says awkwardly, and when I let go of him, I can see his lips tipping up into a curious grin. "Is everything okay?"

Brett answers quickly. "Yeah, everything is cool, man, I was just passing by. You're a lucky guy." He claps Donnie's broad shoulder and walks away with his tail between his legs.

A little about Donnie. He's 6'3, has an athletic build, and is incredibly handsome—all great perks when needing to ward off pushy guys at the club. Before I met him two years ago, I used to pretend Morgan was my girlfriend, but that didn't seem to scare guys off. *Gross*. I can't even count the number of times we got threesome propositions from guys who swore up and down they could turn us straight with their skills in the bedroom.

Donnie looks at me and laughs as he sets our drinks on the table. "So, what was it this time?" He adds a seductive flare to his voice. "Was it your chocolate brown eyes twinkling from across the room, the butterfly tattoo on your shoulder playing peek-a-boo beneath your beautiful blonde hair, or those soft, kissable lips that would tempt even the most faithful man?"

I glare at Donnie, because he knows all of those are reasons that guys—married men, even—have given for feeling compelled to approach me and shoot their shot. I'll admit, the compliments are flattering sometimes, but most of the time, I pick up the vibe that the end game is just to get me home and send me packing once they've got what they wanted, and I'm not about that. I'm not a virgin, but for me, sex is not casual; I have to see a future with that person.

"Are you trying to get smacked?" I chuckle and Donnie raises his hands to surrender.

We start sipping our drinks, and halfway through, Donnie gets this mischievous look in his dark, green eyes.

I narrow mine and ask, "What are you thinking?"

"I just had a good idea."

"Why don't I believe you?" I ask, and he gives me a contemptuous look. "What? I'm just saying, I know what your face looks like when you have a good idea, and the look on your face right now tells me you know I'm going to protest."

"I think you'll change your mind," he says with a confident smile on his light-skinned face. He's probably right. He shares my sense of adventure and love for spontaneity, so it doesn't usually take a whole lot of convincing before my mind is changed. I remember this one time when I had the absolute worst week at work, and Donnie showed up at my apartment door Friday morning with a packed suitcase and told me to call in sick and pack my bags, because we were going on a road trip. For that whole weekend, my face was stitched with a smile and my heart was full. He knew what I needed, and we just went for it. It's the most spontaneous—and rejuvenating—trip we've ever taken together.

He continues, "Okay, I may be a little under the influence right now, but that little fake boyfriend charade gave me an idea."

"If you suggest we should be friends with benefits, I swear I'm going to imprint my palm on your cheek."

He choke laughs on his drink. "Whoa, killer, I'm not *that* drunk. But you *are* in the right vicinity." I tilt my head with curiosity, and he continues. "Okay, so you know how you're heartbroken that I'm leaving you in a week to go on vacation?"

"Yes!" I pout dramatically and cross my arms. I'm a mix of jealous and sad that he'll be in Punta Cana celebrating his brother's wedding and a family vacation for two long weeks—my roommate, Morgan, is also out of town for the next few weeks on a business trip, so I'll be absolutely on my own. "This will be the longest amount of time that we've ever been apart. What if you come back and you can't handle my energy anymore? I would die if I had to find a new best friend to have adventures with."

Donnie and I met two years ago on a trip to Colorado with mutual friends. I'm totally a morning person, so every morning at about 7 a.m., I would wake up full of energy and be ready to go out and kayak, or hike, or do yoga, or something. Anything but lay around waiting for everyone to come alive— it's dreadful.

At about 7:30, my patience would wear off, and I'd start jumping on beds, trying to wake people up, and getting well-deserved pillows tossed at my face. But Donnie was the only one who would actually wake up, get out of bed, and do things with me. And surprisingly, he wasn't even annoyed by my annoying early-bird antics. Although, I totally would have understood if he was. That whole week, we'd go out and do things together before everyone else got up and around. And we've been inseparable ever since.

"Hey." He wraps me in his arms, and I let my head fall against his muscular chest. "You're so dramatic. You know that, right?" He scoffs. "Your energy and zest for life is what I'll always love about you." His compliment makes me smile. "But I was thinking. What if you came on vacation with me?"

I lift my head up and look him in the eyes, wearing a cautious but excited grin, because I would love nothing more than to do exactly that. "Really?"

"Yeah…really."

I squeal happily and then turn it down a bit. "Wait, why do I feel like there's a catch?"

He takes a sip of his drink and rubs his stubbled face with an innocent look in his eyes that is anything but. "Because there is…" He cringes. "I need you to pretend to be my girlfriend."

My eyes widen, and I exclaim, "Wait, what? Why?" I can tell my reaction makes him feel so awkward for even asking, because he's getting all fidgety and dodging my eyes now.

I mean, it's not actually a new concept, because all of our friends—especially Morgan—tell us we would make a cute couple. But our connection has never been romantic—we're affectionate, yes, and playful, but that's just us. I'll admit, we've gone as far as talking about it, but we agreed that just because the attraction and chemistry is there, it doesn't mean we have to cross the friendship line and start dating. Especially because right now, our views on relationships are pretty different; I want my happily ever after and, unfortunately, he's not sure he believes it exists anymore.

"Because I've been sort of dreading this trip. I know that with my brother getting married, my mom is going to start up with the when-are-you-going-to-settle-down-and-find-a-nice-girl conversation every chance she gets. And I mean, I can handle it for a couple days when I visit home for the holidays, but I'm not trying to hear it over the course of two weeks. I just want to enjoy myself."

"Umm, I love you, and trust me, I want to help you, but no way, Donnie. Your parents love me. What happens if they find out we're faking it and they start hating me for lying to them? I couldn't live with that."

"Kase, they won't find out. Like you said, they love you. And because of that, they'll have blinders on when I tell them we're dating. You know, every time I visit home for the holidays, my mom asks me when I'm going to make you my girlfriend. Trust me, when she hears I'm dating you, she won't even dare to question it. I mean, think about it for a second; she'll be happy because I'm dating again, I'll be happy because I can hang out in peace, and you'll be happy because you won't be here in Cali all by yourself for two long and lonely weeks without the most exciting person in your life."

I roll my eyes and take a deep breath while Donnie looks at me like a puppy dog with his stupid, pretty eyes that I have a problem saying no to.

He interlocks his fingers and says, "Pleeeeaaassseee. You'd be the best, best friend in the whole world."

"Ugh," I groan. "You suck." He smiles from ear to ear, and I shake my head. "And, by the way, I am *already* the best, best friend in the whole world. But I'm just letting you know, right now, if I do this, you better be ready to sell the shit out of our relationship, like Oscar-worthy performances, because I will not have your family hating me if we're not believable. I want them to be so convinced we're together that they think we're going to get married."

"Easy! Careful with that word. I don't need you speaking it into existence."

I shove his shoulder. "Hey, don't act like you didn't used to believe in love. I know eventually you'll find the right girl who makes you believe again. But until you find her, you're stuck with me." My lips quirk up into an innocent smile. If I'm being honest though—and maybe a little selfish—I'm kind of glad Donnie doesn't date, because I'm afraid of how it'll change our friendship when the right girl *does* come along. Especially if she doesn't approve of us being so close. That's why most of the guys I've tried dating since I met Donnie have never stuck around. They can't handle me being so close to another guy, so either they leave, or I end it. And that's okay because while I *want* love, I don't *need* it. I just hope Donnie feels the same if he ever finds someone.

"Yeah, I guess there are worse things in the world to be stuck with than you." He shrugs nonchalantly and finishes the rest of his drink.

I gasp. "That is so mean! You better come and dance with me before I change my mind."

"One more drink?"

"Nope, now." I giggle and pull him to the dance floor against his will.

One week later...

~ Day 1, Sunday ~

I am all nerves this morning. I love traveling, but I hate flying. It's the one thing that still, without fail, makes my anxiety flare up. It scares the shit out of me, being so high in the air and putting my life in someone else's hands. I've always preferred to drive wherever I go. I don't care what the statistics say. At least when I'm driving, I have a perceived amount of control over what happens to me.

I've been sitting in this uncomfortable airport chair, alone and tapping my foot nervously for like fifteen minutes now, waiting for Donnie to get back from the bathroom.

Come on, Donnie. How long does it take to pee?

"Okay, this is for you," Donnie's voice says from behind me, and suddenly comfort flows alongside the blood in my veins. When he comes into view, he's got this bright, white smile and two drinks—that I hope are filled with alcohol—extended my way.

"Aww, Donnie." I put my hands over my fluttering heart. "Wait, where's yours?"

"It's okay, I know how nervous you get when we fly. Drink up. They're doubles. We've got a long flight. I mean, it won't be *that* long, but it's…uh—"

I laugh at him trying to backpedal to make it

seem like our flight isn't a long one. It's sweet because I know he's just trying to make me feel at ease, and it's working, to a degree.

He takes a seat next to me and wraps his arm around me after I grab the drinks. I swear I could cry right now. He's such an attentive friend. "Thank you. If we die today, just know that I love you."

He chuckles softly and ignores that my voice is loud enough that our seat neighbors turn their heads.

Oops, probably not the best language to use in an airport.

"Kasie, we're not going to die today. All right? Before you know it, we'll be sipping piña coladas out of real coconuts instead of airport tequila sunrise's out of plastic cups. Okay?"

I try to hide the uncertainty on my face as I look at the confidence on his. I nod to appease him and start drinking until I believe him.

Chapter Two

Donnie

We made it. And Kasie couldn't look more thrilled. The energy and giddiness I'm used to seeing from her is finally returning now that we've landed. And so is the sun-kissed glow of her dewy skin.

She looks at me and I grin, not daring to say, 'I told you so,' but she must already know what I'm thinking because she softly smacks my forearm. "Don't even. We made it safely *this* time."

"Just like we do *every* time."

She gives me a dirty look, but I see a small quirk of her lips hiding beneath it. We travel together quite a bit. Sometimes just me and her, but mostly with our group of friends. We usually have to find places within driving distance because flying gives her anxiety. But every now and then, I use my charm to convince her that flying gives us the opportunity to go somewhere completely strange and new. And she *loves* strange and new.

We get off the plane, claim our luggage, and get on the bus that takes us to our resort, Enchanted Shores.

"This place is ridiculous," I exclaim, marveling at the sugar-white sand and sprawling palm trees lining the three-story resort that looks like a luxurious Caribbean palace. We check in and walk the marbled floors that lead to our first-floor suite. When we step inside, I look over at Kasie just in time to see her jaw drop and her pretty brown eyes light up. She shoves her suitcase against the wall and starts exploring the room; I follow behind her, her awe mirroring my own. A big, flatscreen TV is mounted to the living room wall opposite a large white couch with turquoise throw pillows that match the ocean we can see just beyond our floor-to-ceiling windows. The patio doors open up to a seating area and steps down to our private infinity pool that looks straight out to the ocean.

Now this is paradise.

"This trip is going to be one for the memory books," I holler loud enough for Kasie to hear in the next room. "I can feel it."

Aside from being excited to paint Punta Cana red with my best friend for the next two weeks, I'm happy to witness my brother, Connor, finally tying the knot with the girl of his dreams, his high school sweetheart, Mila. They haven't had an easy road, but they stuck together and made it through every obstacle. I admire how strong their bond is, and it's because of those two that my non-believer ass still holds on to a sliver of hope that love may someday still be in the cards for me. But right now, I'm enjoying the single life—something I really never got to do before, because I always thought I had to be with someone.

Being alone used to scare me, but not anymore. I'm happy. There's no strings in my life—no drama, no jealousy…all that shit that comes with being tied to someone.

"Oh my gosh! Donnie, the view from our bedroom patio is amazing!" Kasie hollers from the bedroom. "Come check it out. Oh, and I forgot to grab our glasses of wine from the counter. Can you bring them in, please?"

"Hold on, when and how did you get wine already?"

"There's a wine dispenser by the

refrigerator. Can you believe it? We've never stayed somewhere with our own personal wine dispenser. So fancy! There's like, four different types of wine to choose from. Ahh, I could totally live here."

I smile to myself, grab the wine from the counter, and meet her in the bedroom, where she's standing at the patio door. She turns and looks at me with a big, giddy, wholesome smile as I approach the patio door to gaze out at the lapping ocean waves. I go to hand her the wine, but she doesn't take it yet.

Instead, she moves to the king-sized bed, falls back onto it, and sprawls out. "I call dibs on the bed, by the way."

"Wait, what?"

"Of course, I'll let you check it out and see how lavish and soft it is, but when it's nighttime, your ass is going to have to cuddle up on the couch. You know I'm bougie; I can't sleep out there." She smirks, and I furrow my brows at her, handing her the glass of wine, although, I *should* set it on the dresser and make her get it herself for claiming rights to the bed already.

She's lucky I love her—and owe her big

time for agreeing to be my fake girlfriend—so I don't put up a fuss. "Anyways," I say dramatically, "my family will be here anytime. Should we go over ground rules or something to make sure we're on the same page with this boyfriend-girlfriend shit?"

"I mean, I don't know what we would need to go over. We just have to do everything a normal boyfriend and girlfriend would do, right?" She pauses and looks amused. "You *do* remember how to do that, don't you?" She giggles.

I shake my head. "You're lucky you have a drink in your hand."

"Oh yeah? What are you going to do if I set it down?" She gets a competitive look in her eyes and scoots back towards the headboard to lean over and set her wine glass on the nightstand, smirking her cherry lips.

Kasie is small, but you'd never know it by the way she competes.

I set my wine down as well and then reach for her leg to pull her toward me but she's quick, and all I grab is air. She laughs and stands to her feet, bouncing back and forth in the middle of the bed with her hands up like an MMA fighter. I move to the bottom edge of the bed and grab hold of the comforter, ready to pull it out from under her.

Kasie's eyes widen. "Don't you dare!" She points a stern finger at me, but I've already decided she's going down.

Before she can react, I pull the comforter out and she yelps as she lands on her back like a turtle, her head is surrounded by a sea of blonde hair. I hop on the bed, pin her down, and within seconds she's laughing uncontrollably while I tickle the sides of her stomach and just above her knees.

When she taps out, I release her and she rolls to her side, panting.

"That was so not fair," she groans. "You just wait, I'm going to get you back when you least expect it."

My text alert goes off, and I reach in my pocket to slide my phone out. It's my brother.

[Connor]: "What's up, broski!? We just landed. Get pretty and shit, because Mom and Dad want us to meet for lunch at The Enchanted Tiki at 2."

[Me]: "Cool, bro. We'll be there. You better be ready to drink today, you old-ass."

Connor is 27—3 years older than me—and we've always been close. Most older brothers would rather eat dirt than have their younger brother following their every move. But not Connor. He took the role of 'big brother' very seriously.

Growing up, I learned a lot from him. Mostly, how to not be a shitty baseball player. But he also taught me how to fight, how to shotgun a beer, how to talk to girls, and the list goes on. Teaching has always been his forte, which is why I wasn't surprised a bit when he accepted the head coaching position for our hometown high school baseball team after Coach Henry passed away last summer. Aside from my breakup with Olivia, last summer was one of the roughest times of my life. Coach was like a second father to me, and it killed me that the last time I had seen him was the Christmas before he passed. I was so broken up that, at his funeral, I couldn't even finish the speech I wrote. Thankfully, I had Kasie by my side, and she was able to finish it for me. I don't know what I would do without that girl.

"All right, we've got an hour," I tell Kasie.

"They want to meet up for lunch. Want to freshen up and hit one of the lounges before they get here?"

Her eyes light up. "Umm, yes!" She jumps off the bed and starts unpacking her bag to put everything away. She cannot stand to live out of a suitcase when we travel. I used to think she was weird for hanging stuff up and folding things away and all that, but she eventually converted me. I'll admit that it *is* more convenient knowing where things are rather than digging through an unorganized suitcase.

We finish putting our things away and I style my hair while she teases hers. When she's finished, she turns to me and asks, "So, do I look like the girl next door that you'd bring home to your mom or am I showing too much skin?"

She twirls around to show me her whole outfit. She's wearing a white tank top that shows her toned stomach and a pair of ripped jean shorts. "I think you look gorgeous, Kase. Don't worry, my parents aren't *that* old-school."

"Okay, good. Because these shorts make my ass look perky and cute. Oh, and before we go, there's just one thing left to do."

"What's that?"

"Kiss me."

I scoff and about spit my wine out, but Kasie's face is stone-cold serious. "Kiss you? Why... what... How?"

"Oh my gosh, like take your lips and press them against mine. Kiss me. Look, you know we're going to have to, and the first kiss is going to be the most awkward one because we've never done this before. So, let's just get it out of the way while we're alone, that way we can be awkward about it and hopefully all the other ones will look like we actually enjoy kissing each other."

Hmm, she brings up a good point. To be honest, I hadn't even thought about all the things we'd have to do to sell our relationship, I was just ecstatic that she said yes.

She puts her hands on her hips and continues. "Trust me, I don't like it any more than you do, but you're the one who signed us up for this, remember?" She grins.

I sigh, rubbing my palm across my jaw. "Yeah, yeah. All right, fine. You're right. Let's do it. I mean, kiss. Let's kiss, not do it. Fuck! You know what I mean."

She giggles and then steps towards me, giving me this alluring look, which only adds to the awkwardness. And why is it so quiet in here now?

"What's wrong, Donnie?" she says with a tone that is just as alluring as the way she's staring me down. "Do I make you nervous?" She looks down at the ground and then back up at me, blinking sweetly.

Damn, she's good. The little hairs on the back of my neck are standing up.

"Uh, are you trying to be sexy or something?" I laugh quietly as I step back a bit.

"Shut up, I'm trying to get into character. Now, come on. Be serious."

"Okay, let's start again."

I take a deep breath, step toward her, and my heart rate takes off.

Okay, how should I do this?

If we *were* dating, I would focus on the softness behind her eyes before I lean in, but they're too familiar, so I can't linger there. I move my gaze to her also-familiar lips and try to look at them like they've never been planted on my forehead after she's cheered me up during one of my emo moments. And then I focus on her bottom lip, remembering the time her drunk ass ran into the bathroom door and busted it.

Uh, this isn't working.

"I can't do it when you're looking at me like that."

"Like what?"

"Like... I don't know, just—"

"Ok, fine, here, I'll close my eyes." She squeezes her eyes shut and giggles. "I feel like I'm fourteen, having my first kiss again."

"Wait, you were fourteen when you had your first kiss?"

She opens her eyes back up. "Yeah, how old were you?"

I rub my shoulder, and my tone turns a bit sheepish, "Fifteen."

"Really?" Her eyes widen. "Weren't you a baseball star, though? I figured all the girls would have been throwing themselves at you. I've seen the throwback pictures of you in those tight baseball pants. You've always had that strong jawline and those broody eyes. I'm not going to lie; I totally would have been a groupie."

"I'm flattered. But, no, I did have girls trying to get at me, I just had tunnel vision for Cecilia Ruiz. I remember when I got home that day after having my first kiss with her, I thought I'd found the one."

"Aww, so what happened?"

"Well, turns out I wasn't the only one that she liked kissing. So, I ended it and spent the remainder of my high school career jumping from relationship to relationship, trying to find someone that made me feel the same way she did."

And I didn't find that until my sophomore year in college, when I met Olivia—my most recent ex, who shattered my heart three years ago. She had never been on my radar in high school, because, she was quiet, and I wasn't. She was also a childhood family friend, so it just never felt like an option until we ended up in the same history class in college. Eventually, we kissed, and what I felt all those years ago with Cecilia, I felt again but with

Olivia.

"Oh, well, her loss then."

The compliment warms my cheeks. "Yeah, you're right."

"Aren't I always?" Kasie smirks, and I roll my eyes.

"Ok, so, are you ready?"

"Yep. Let's both close our eyes though. You can picture me as Megan Fox. It shouldn't be hard to imagine kissing *her* since you're so obsessed with her."

I chuckle. "I am not."

She side-eyes me. "You totally are. What is it that you say every time you see her on the screen?" She makes her voice sound like what I'm guessing is supposed to be her version of my low voice, "'Damn, look at those lips, Kasie. They look so plump and soft. With just one kiss, she could make me believe in love again.'"

"That's not even how I sound."

"Yes, it is."

I laugh. "You are so lame." She smiles proudly at the jab and I ask, "Okay, so, if I'm picturing you as Megan Fox, who are you going to picture me as?"

"Easy. Chris Hemsworth. He's as tall and muscular as you are. He's usually got a little more scruff going on than you, but I can imagine he just finished showering and is going with a clean stubble or something."

"That's oddly specific…"

I brace for her punch, but surprisingly it doesn't come.

"Just shut up and kiss me already, so we can go have drinks before your family gets here."

"All right, all right."

I step inside her bubble space again, close my eyes, and lean down, touching my lips to hers. She's kissed my forehead and cheeks before, so I knew she had soft lips, but damn if there's not something different about them when they're pressed against mine. It's kind of throwing me.

Shit.

I'm just now realizing, we never discussed how long this kiss was supposed to last. Is it a quick kiss on top of the lips? Are we making out? How do I know when to stop? I don't want to make this weirder by going further than she expects.

*D*amn, *I've got to get better at thinking things through.*

She must be able to read my mind because she answers my questions by linking her arms around my neck to pull me further into the kiss.

Okay, we're making out.

I erase Kasie's face from my head and replace her with Megan Fox, but the fruity, aromatic floral scent of her perfume that I know so well invades my nose and threatens to spoil Megan's image from my mind. I fight the image of Kasie replacing Megan and gently bite down on her plump bottom lip. I massage her tongue with mine, stealing her breath until it grows heavy against mine. This feels hot, thrilling, and wrong, all at the same time. Once Megan is slated in my mind, I turn on autopilot and slowly walk Kasie back against the wall. It's been a long time since I've kissed someone so deeply. So long that I'm starting to get hard, and now I feel guilty for enjoying this.

Fuck, go back down.

But I should know better. The more I try to fight it, the harder I'm getting.

You have to stop, Kasie. Because I can't.

But she doesn't. Her hands are wrapped around my neck and head, keeping me close. I should just pull away, but I'm stuck. It's like sleep paralysis, but I guess kiss paralysis? I don't even know if that's a thing, but she just made it one. When I feel her grip loosen, I get my bearings back and break away. Before she notices the bulge in my jeans, I hurry to the living room.

"Are you okay?" she calls out after me.

"Yeah, I'm fine," I holler back, trying to focus on anything that will soften me before she comes out here. "I just had this bad feeling that I lost my wallet at the airport." The excuse sucks, but it'll have to do, because the only other thing on my mind is how I shouldn't have enjoyed that kiss as much as I did.

No, you know what? It's not weird. Yeah, I'm not supposed to like kissing my best friend, but she's beautiful, so of course I'm going to like kissing a beautiful girl. It would be weird if I didn't.

So, it's not a big deal. It's not like anything changes between us just because I enjoyed a kiss. I don't even know why I'm so hung up on it. It was just a kiss. It's fine. Everything is fine.

"Hey." Her voice makes me jump a bit. "Woah, you're like, super jumpy. Are you sure you're ok?"

"Yeah, I'm good. I was spaced out. Found my wallet, by the way. Everything is good."

"O…kay," she says, wearing a skeptical look on her face.

"Really, I'm fine. Let's go drink, weirdo."

"You're the weird one." She shoves me, and we laugh as we head for the door.

Real smooth, Donnie. Real smooth.

Chapter Three

Kasie

Donnie and I choose an outdoor bar by a huge pool with crystal water that's full of people sipping on pretty drinks and golden beer. The sun is kissing our skin while a gentle breeze wraps around us, rustling the overhead palm trees. I listen to the sound of ocean waves lapping and breathe in the salty sea air, wishing my painted toes were buried in warm, white sand right now. But I suppose I can settle for sipping on a piña colada out of a coconut with my best friend.

"I cannot believe they're getting married out here. It's so romantic." I sigh happily. "I love love."

I'm the type of girl who still believes in fairy tales, true love, and all that cheesy romantic stuff that makes people roll their eyes. And they can keep on rolling them, because cheesy or not, love makes my heart so fucking happy. And I'm thankful that even though Donnie doesn't believe in love anymore, he doesn't trash my hopes of finding it one day.

And about a year ago, I thought I *had* found it. With Liam. He was so good to me, and the sex was good, too, but then he got a promotion at work, and it took over his life. So, eventually, after I'd had enough of being neglected, I made the decision to leave him. I was heartbroken, but I'm pretty sure my recovery time was cut in half thanks to the breakup party that Donnie and Morgan threw me. It was as entertaining as it was empowering. And after it, I knew I had made the right decision.

"Would your dream wedding be in a place like this?"

"My dream wedding? No, it's breathtaking out here, but I always imagined a wedding in the French countryside next to a beautiful chateau. I'd get married in the middle of a big, colorful garden, backdropped by pretty, green trees. They'd be speckled with pastel colored décor to match the tables. I would be dripping in sparkly jewelry, wearing a strapless mermaid dress. I'd dance the night away in a decorated ballroom." I adopt a haughty English accent. "It would be the most elegant affair in all the land." I giggle.

"Oh, I don't doubt that. So, do I get to be a bridesmaid in this elegant affair?" Donnie asks.

"Umm, the correct term is bridesman. But, no, if I was getting married today, you'd be my man of honor."

"That's a thing?"

"Yeah, it actually is."

"Hmm." He presses his index finger against his chin, like he's pondering whether he would accept or not. It's kind of cute that he thinks he could say no in the first place. "Well, you know what? I would love to be your man of honor."

"Good, because you don't have a choice," I deadpan, leaning my shoulder into his.

We finish our drinks and have time for one more before he gets a text telling us everyone is at the tiki restaurant across the way.

Here we go.

We pay our tabs, and I wrap my arms lovingly around his biceps as we walk the outdoor path leading to the restaurant. Side note: I don't know what cologne he is wearing, but it's new and damn, he smells kind of sexy.

When we get there, the restaurant is everything I expected plus more. The patio area where it is located is surrounded by tiki torches, and every table has a tiki umbrella opened up above it. The waitresses are walking around in coconut bikini tops—which I hope I can find in a shop somewhere around here because I totally need one—and hula skirts. To complement their tropical shorts, the waiters are shirtless, full of tattoos and muscles, and wearing colorful leis around their necks. And to top it off, there's a live band in the corner of the restaurant playing island music, which makes me miss Morgan. She is one busy girl, always entertaining high-end clients. But every other week, we carve out a day to have a girl's lunch date, and we make it a mission to visit somewhere that plays live music, because that's our thing. There's something about it that soothes our restless souls.

Donnie and I reach the wooden, circular table where his family is gathered, and he does something no other guy has ever done for me—like ever—not even him: he pulls out my chair and waits for me to take my seat before taking his. I smile, trying not to act like it's the first time this has ever happened, because we're supposed to have been dating for a few months now.

"Thank you, baby," I say, taking my seat and feeling special, even though I know he only did it to keep up appearances.

I haven't seen everyone in person since I traveled to Donnie's hometown—Smoky Valley, Michigan—for his coach's funeral last year. It was heartbreaking, but we did end up having some good moments in between the sad ones. I finally got to meet his whole family, we all went camping together—I've been itching to do it again ever since—and Donnie took me to Miss Dee's General Store and got me hooked on her homemade taffy. I make sure he gets some for me now every time he visits home for Thanksgiving and Christmas.

And I met Mila, Connor's fiancée. She was so genuine and fun to be around. She was even sweet enough to teach me how to make sticky rice and this spicy and sour dipping sauce that I became obsessed with, Jeow Som. I'm happy to know her mom is making *that* and some other traditional Laotian foods for the wedding.

We make it to the table, and Mila snaps up from her seat and welcomes me with open arms.

"Girl, how do you stay so fucking gorgeous all the time?" she asks, giving me a onceover.

"Oh, please, have you seen yourself?"

Aside from her porcelain skin, Mila has pretty, almond-shaped, dark brown eyes, and the silkiest black hair I've ever seen in my life. The girl is beautiful.

She laughs, and I make my rounds, hugging Charlotte—Donnie's mom—who's no taller than I am but her presence makes Hank—Donnie's dad—seem like the short one, although he's definitely not. Donnie and Connor each get their height and broad shoulders from him. And I'm reminded when Charlotte smiles at me that Donnie has her smile. It's pretty on her, but on him? Be still my heart.

After ordering our food and drinks, Charlotte's smile turn curious. "You know, I have been trying to get this boy to make a move on you for a long time now, and each time I did, he swears up and down it wouldn't happen. No doubt I am happy as a clam at high tide, but I must wonder. What did you do to change this stubborn boy's mind?"

Oh, shit. What did I do? We haven't even

thought of a backstory. Dang, we are so bad at this.

I think for a second and just run with the first thing that comes to my mind. "I got drunk," I say plainly, and everyone widens their eyes, including Donnie, who's probably now regretting asking me to play this part. I laugh and put my hands up. "Let me explain. There was this one day, after Donnie and I spent all afternoon and evening at the San Diego County Fair, I realized that I was falling for the way he smiles at me. I started longing for his company when he wasn't around. Not like, I-miss-my-best-friend kind of longing but like I-need-you-to-feel-complete kind of longing. So, one night, I worked up a little alcohol courage and asked him if he would be willing to give me and him a chance. I told him we don't have to fall in love, let's just see where it goes."

I turn to look at Donnie, and the doting boyfriend look in his eyes is plenty convincing. I smile and tuck a strand of hair behind my ear, betting he's impressed with my improv skills. He takes my hand in his and rubs the back of it with his thumb, smiling gently at me. It's kind of an awkward feeling staring so deep into my best friend's eyes, but at the same time, I feel so welcomed and at home there. He's my safe place.

It isn't until Connor booms "Get a room!" that I realize how long we must have been lost in the moment.

My cheeks turn pink, and Donnie laughs nervously before changing the subject. "Bro, you do realize I'm the one in charge of the best-man speech, right?"

"Yeah, and you better say some good shit. I want tears streaming from my face, man."

Mila smacks his arm lightheartedly. "In that case, I want tears streaming from your face while I'm walking down the aisle, too."

"Pumpkin, as soon as you step out in that beautiful wedding dress, there won't be a dry eye within fifty feet of you, especially mine."

Aww, he calls her pumpkin.

I love cute nicknames. I tried convincing Donnie to let me call him sweet cheeks while we're out here, but he wasn't having it. He usually gives in to my sad face, but he held strong against that one.

"Dude, you're the sensitive one, of course you're going to cry," Donnie jests and then winces as Connor punches his arm.

"I may be more in tune with my emotions, but I'll still kick your ass."

"Well, I'll tell you what, this mama is going to need help holding it together." Charlotte's voice is a soft rasp, as if she may actually cry right now. "I can't believe my first-born baby is getting married."

"Aww, Mom," Connor says, rubbing his mother's hand from across the table. "What about you, Pops? Do you think you'll have some waterworks going?" he asks.

Donnie scoffs. "Yeah, right. I don't even think dad's tear ducts work."

Everyone cracks up and Hank creases his brows. "Now, hold on just a second. I've cried before."

"Did you document it, Pop? Because I don't believe you unless I see some proof," Donnie says, looking unconvinced. I'm kind of with him on that, though. Everything I know about Hank suggests that the first and only time he cried was when he was born.

"Well, son," Hank says, looking at Donnie sternly, "Do you remember when you went off to college and decided you'd live in the dorms instead of at home?"

"Yeah, I remember. Wait a minute, you cried when I moved out?" Donnie's eyes widen.

"Oh, no. I cried when you told us your dorm wasn't ready yet, so your mother and I had to wait another week before finally having the house all to ourselves."

Everyone at the table bursts into laughter, and Hank grins proudly.

Donnie shakes his head and takes a defeated sip of his beer. "Damn, Dad, I see how it is. Okay, well, you just wait until we get on the golf course tomorrow. I'm not taking it easy on you. I've been working on my game."

"Oh, don't worry," I pipe up, ready to join in on roasting Donnie. "I was with him the last time he went golfing. I don't know much about golf, but I'm pretty sure hanging your head after every putt isn't a good sign."

Donnie drops his jaw and looks at me like he's starstruck. It's actually kind of cute. Like it makes me want to bear hug him with comforting arms, even though I know he's joking. "Wow, babe, it's like that?"

I sweeten my smile and give him a half-shrug as Mila says, "Oh, Kasie, before I forget. While the guys are out golfing tomorrow, Charlotte and I are getting spa mani-pedis. Please tell me you'll come too?" She looks at me like I'd break her heart if I said no, which I wouldn't, because I would never turn down a spa day.

"Of course. I am so down!"

Our waiter stops by with our food, a second round of drinks, and the rum shots for each of us that Donnie ordered a bit ago. After we clink our glasses and shoot back our rum, I can feel a little buzz starting to set in.

As another small talk conversation begins, a couple screaming with excitement—or maybe terror—grabs everyone's attention. The couple are strapped to a colorful parachute a few hundred feet in the air, being pulled by a boat speeding across the ocean waves. It looks like so much fun, and I am only just now wondering why I've never done that before.

I'm watching, totally transfixed, when Donnie interrupts my hopefully gazing. "You want to go, don't you?"

"Would you go with me?"

"Hmmm," he says, rubbing his chin as everyone at the table seems to be waiting on his answer.

"Come on, please don't make me beg," I say, giving him the sweetest, most innocent look I can muster, hoping it'll sway his decision in my favor.

"You know what, it scares the hell out of me, but of course, I'll go with you."

I squeal with excitement. "Ahhhh, you're the best!" I squeeze my arms around his neck.

I hope he's being for real and not just saying it to keep up appearances.

Could I go by myself? Of course, but I love sharing experiences like that with the people who mean the most to me.

When I let him go, he leans in and kisses the side of my head. It makes me smile. Like *legitimately* smile. His gentle kiss warms me up and makes me feel like all giddy inside. He's really good at playing this loving boyfriend role. Better than I expected. Although, I'm still wondering why he rushed out of the room so quickly after we kissed earlier. I'm pretty sure he wasn't actually worried about his wallet. I mean, I knew the kiss was going to be awkward. We both did. But I thought we would at least talk about it afterward to help ease the awkwardness a little. But since we didn't, it's kind of left this weird vibe lingering in the air, and I can't tell what it is. I've been ignoring it, but—I don't know.

Maybe it's just me. Maybe this is just how it feels when you kiss your best friend with tongue. I didn't really expect it to be so passionate, it just kind of…happened. I blame Megan Fox and Chris Hemsworth.

"I love how you guys are always so fucking down to do things together," Mila says after she takes a sip of her cocktail. "Like, you have so many cool-ass memories as best friends, but it's nice to see that you haven't changed just because you started dating."

"Yeah," Connor chimes in while cutting into

his steak. "A lot of couples do that and lose the spark that brought them together. But if you guys just keep vibing with each other, it only gets better from here, because there are some memories that only couples can make."

He looks up and smiles at me before taking a bite of his steak. Everyone is so happy for Donnie and me that it makes me feel bad for lying to them. But I have to keep it together, because there is no way I am letting anyone at this table find out that Donnie and I are frauds. I may be grown enough to not need *everyone's* approval anymore, but I *do* need my best friend's family's approval.

After lunch, Mila, Connor, Donnie, and I make plans to check out the swimming pool in an hour while Charlotte and Hank decide to relax in their room before our dinner and tequila tasting later this evening.

At the pool, Donnie and Connor grab bright

white pool chairs while Mila and I sit with our feet in the sparkling water, sipping on frozen tropical drinks. Connor takes a seat next to Mila and gives her a sweet kiss on the cheek that makes her light up. My heart dances in my chest as I watch them; they're so happy.

I can't wait to have that.

Donnie takes his seat next to me, removes his tank top, and tosses it back on our pool chair.

"Show off." Connor rolls his eyes. "You know, my abs used to look like that."

"Yeah, until all the meat and potatoes caught up with you." Mila laughs, patting her hand on Connor's stomach. "It's okay, honey, I like your dad-bod."

"But I'm not even a dad, yet... Wait a minute! Or are you announcing something right now?"

"Baby, I just took shots at lunch, I'm obviously not pregnant," she says, and it makes Donnie and I laugh. "But, you know, we *do* have two weeks to try." She nudges his arm, and he leans in, rubbing her nose with his.

"Hey, you guys remember that room that you were suggesting Kasie and I should get earlier? It's all yours," Donnie says drily.

My phone rings, interrupting the moment. It's my dad. I get up and walk out of earshot to take the call, because I am not about to fake our relationship to him too.

My dad loves Donnie as much as Donnie's family loves me. He's visited me in California numerous times since I moved, and he first met Donnie during a Lakers game. It was an important game, too—the Lakers vs the Bulls. My dad's team is the Chicago Bulls. But me? I've always liked the Lakers and not just because I had a huge crush on Kobe—*rest in peace to the legend.*

I actually understand the game because it was our "thing" ever since I was a little girl. He would get this big, blue mixing bowl out, fill it with popcorn, and we'd sit on the couch watching Chicago Bulls re-runs until my little eyes got too heavy and I'd fall asleep. Initially, I was only interested in the popcorn and quality time. But eventually, I started understanding the game and began cheering along. When my dad realized his little girl was really interested in watching basketball, we started watching the live games on TV together. Although, he was devastated when I decided I liked the Lakers instead of the Bulls, but hey, I liked their colors better. And thank goodness I ended up picking a winning team, because it made for some lucrative bets when I got older.

"Hey, Daddy!" I greet cheerfully.

"Hi, sweet pea. I just wanted to check in and see how your trip is going, since you forgot to let me know you made it safely."

"Oops!" I smack my forehead. "I'm sorry. I guess I was just so relieved when we touched down that it slipped my mind."

"You're okay. So, how is it?"

"This place is so beautiful! Oh my gosh, you would love it. We just had lunch, and now we're swimming in one of the huge pools this place has. Everything is going great. What about you, did Sheila show up?"

"She did. She's nice, pretty, and even convinced me to go on a second date."

"Yay! I hope it works out. You deserve it."

"Thank you. We'll see what happens. Well, I'll let you get back to your vacation. I just wanted to make sure you made it there safely. Tell Donnie I said hello and to keep you out of trouble." I can hear the grin in his voice.

"Hey, I'm the innocent one."

My dad just chuckles. "I love you, sweet pea."

"I love you too, Daddy."

I tap the end call button and look up to see Donnie gazing my way. I smile softly, tucking my hair behind my ear, as this bashful feeling floats around in my stomach when he smiles after me. I sigh happily.

I love my life.

Chapter Four

Donnie

Kasie and I stagger into the room, and I press my back against the door as she stumbles toward the minifridge.

"That last tequila shot hit different, right?" I ask as she tosses me a bottle of water that I'm not coordinated enough to catch right now. It hits the floor with a thud.

"Yes. It was so smooth. I didn't even need a chaser."

"See, I told you you could do it. Shoot it, breathe in through your nose, blow out through your mouth, and you're good. Next up, whiskey shots without a chaser."

"Umm, let's take it one shot at a time." She laughs. "Oh my gosh, your brother had me dying after every shot. The faces he would make; I didn't know he was a horrible shot-taker. Poor Mila, she looked so embarrassed."

"Oh, by now, embarrassing her is a sport to him. There was this one time during my freshman year of high school—his senior year—they were both nominated to the homecoming court. During the announcement of all the couples, they had a chance to walk the aisle in the auditorium together, and they got about halfway down the aisle before he faked a slip and just fell to the floor. Granted, he and the guys had a bet that he wouldn't have the balls to pull it off, but he fucking did it. The whole auditorium roared with laughter. Mila's face was so red. I actually kind of felt bad for her."

Kasie giggles. "That is hilarious…and somehow, brave?"

I plop down on the couch and get comfortable, leaning on the armrest. I stare at the blank TV screen, waiting for the room to stop feeling like I'm on a boat in the ocean. Kasie disappears into the room long enough to put her hair into a ponytail and change into pajama shorts and a big, graphic T-shirt that looks oddly familiar.

"Is that my shirt?" I ask as she lays down on the couch and uses my thigh as a pillow.

"Well, it was. But it's mine now."

I can see a grin forming on her face.

"Yours?"

"Yep. You left it at my place last month. I honestly forgot I still had it until a couple weeks ago when I was looking for something cozy to wear while watching my murder mysteries."

"Wait, I don't remember walking around shirtless in your apartment." I think for a moment and then it comes to me. "Oh shit." I scoff as foggy memories of that shirtless night replay in my head. "That's the night I spilled wine all over myself and your rug."

"Yeah, and the next day, I told you to come get your shirt, but I guess you wanted me to have it. You owe me, anyway, since I couldn't get the stain out."

I laugh to myself and twist the cap off my water to take a gulp. "Fair enough."

We sit in silence for a bit, scrolling through our phones, until Kasie sets hers down.

She inspects her fingernails for a couple

seconds before she says, "You know what we should talk about?"

"What's that?" I ask, setting my phone on the armrest.

"Our kiss."

"What do you mean?" My eyes widen, and my heart thumps as I wonder if she may have saw how hard I was earlier. Or even worse, could she have felt it? I'm pretty sure I backed away in time, but maybe not?

"Well, we didn't really talk about it at all. You just kind of rushed out, and we went on about our day. But I feel like maybe we should have talked about it? I don't know. Is that weird?"

"I don't know. I guess I didn't really think about it since it wasn't a real kiss, you know?"

"Yeah, I know. But it did *really* happen."

I sit up a little straighter and try not to think too deep about the kiss for fear I'll get hard again. And her head is still on my thigh, so I can't think of a worse time for my dick to have a mind of its own. "Ok, well, yeah, I'm down for talking about it. So…what do we talk about?"

"Good question. I guess I didn't really think past suggesting we talk about the kiss…hmm…" She takes a moment and then says, "Okay, I *have* to know. Am I a good kisser?"

"Really?" I scoff. "I feel like that's a question that's going to make this weird."

"What? Why? Donnie, I'm in a unique position. I've never kissed a guy who didn't have something to gain by telling me I'm a good kisser. I'm just curious. I mean, it's not like kissing me changed the way you feel about me, did it?" She lifts her head from my thigh and looks at me with worry in her eyes.

"Oh, no, definitely not." I say quickly, and it must ease her mind because she sighs like she just dodged a bullet and lays her head back down on my leg.

"Good. Me neither. So, answer the question. Am I a good kisser or not?"

"Honestly, you're a great kisser."

"Great? You could have just said good. Now I *do* feel awkward." I see her holding back a smirk, so I move my thigh out from under her head. She cracks up with laughter and snorts as her head falls to the couch cushion.

"You play too much." I shake my head, unable to stop the soft laughter from escaping behind my lips.

She sits up and looks at me, still smiling. "You love it." I give her a jesting glare and she continues. "So, you didn't rush out of the room because of anything I did?"

"No, I really thought I left my wallet at the airport. Nothing to do with you," I lie, and I feel sick for it, but there is no way I am telling her the truth.

She scoots towards me to wrap me in a hug. "Okay, well, I feel much better now. Anyway, I'm going to get some sleep, fake boyfriend. I'll see you bright and early for breakfast and mimosas before we part ways."

I grab the extra blanket from the closet, a fluffy pillow from the bed, tell Kasie goodnight, and setup my sleeping spot on the couch.

A pounding at the door jolts me awake. I run my hand down face and sigh heavily, burying my hands in my hair as I sit up.

Damn, what time is it?

I grab my phonc off the end table to check.

It's midnight, just thirty minutes after I laid down.

I get up to approach the peep hole to figure out who the fuck is banging on our door. It's Connor.

I open the door and he's standing there, cheesing, holding up three bottles of beer.

"Damn, bro, you knock like the police." I let him in and close the door. "I figured your ass would have been passed out by now."

Connor huffs and hands me a beer as he takes a seat at the dining table. "Dude, I don't know what kind of tequila we drank, but I've been wired. Mila was getting tired, so I thought I'd stop by and see what you and Kasie were up to. I was certain you'd still be up drinking or having sex or—" He scans the room, probably looking for Kasie, and then cocks his head to the side. "Wait a minute, did you and Kasie have a fight?"

"A fight? No, why would you think that?"

He points at the couch and gives me a curious look.

Shit.

"Ohhh." I force a small laugh and think of a quick, hopefully believable excuse as I take a seat at the table with him. "No, man. We were just cuddling, watching a movie together, and I must have fallen asleep. I'm always doing that."

"Aww." He puts his hand sarcastically over his heart. "And she brought blankets out here to tuck you in? That's adorable, bro."

"Man, shut up." I shove his shoulder and he laughs.

"Does she hate that shit, though? When you fall asleep during movie time."

"Yeah, man. With a passion."

It's not completely untrue. Every Sunday, Kasie and I have a movie day. We'll go grab a bunch of snacks and popcorn, pick up some drinks, get cozy either at her place or mine, and just binge watch movies all day long. The only problem is, it's inevitable that by the time we get to the late evening movies, I'm fighting to keep my eyes open. We don't argue about it, but she does like to give me shit for not being able to stay awake.

"Mila, too. Sometimes I think she's going to murder me in my sleep." Connor chuckles and twists the cap off of his beer. I open mine, as well, and we clink our bottles together before he says, "I was actually wanting to tell you something, so you're not blindsided when she gets here next week."

"Okay?" I crease my brows, studying his hazel eyes like I may find a clue inside them.

He breathes a harsh breath. "Olivia's coming. I don't know if she'll be here for the bachelorette thing, but her sister will be, so just assume she will too."

My heart drops to my stomach. I haven't seen her since the day I left our hometown under the notion she'd be joining me a couple weeks later.

My eyes glaze over as a flashback of the

phone call I got a week before she was supposed to meet me in San Diego plays in my head.

"What do you mean, you're not coming? I've got everything ready. My job, the apartment—"

"I'm just... I'm not ready, Donnie."

"All right, fine. If you're not ready, I'll just come back, and we can wait until you are. I'm sure Chip still has my spot available, and I can get my money back for the apartment."

"No, Donnie, don't."

"What? Why not?"

"Look, I just think it would be best if we stopped seeing each other. I– I'm sorry."

"Olivia, baby, did I do something wrong? If I did, just tell me, so I can fix it."

"It's not you, okay? It's me. We're young, Donnie. We have our whole lives ahead of us, and I'm just not ready for all of this."

"All of what?"

"Serious relationships. Taking the next step...moving in together. When we started dating,

we were just having fun. I never expected things to get as serious as they have. But then they did, and you were so happy, and I didn't have the heart to tell you things were moving too fast for me."

"We've been together for three years, Olivia."

"And they've been great, but I...it's just too much."

"So, you waited until I was over 2,000 miles away to tell me this?"

"I'm sorry. Truly, I am. But you'll find someone out there who will love you the way you want to be loved. I know you will."

"When was it over for you?"

"Does it really matter?"

"It matters to me."

"Just promise me you'll move on, Donnie."

"Olivia—"

"Promise me. Please."

"No."

"Donnie, please. I need to know—"

I hung up the phone, and that was the last time I spoke to her. It was also the day I stopped believing in happily ever afters. I still remember the sound my phone made that day when it hit the countertop in my empty apartment. It was a lonely echo that reminded me I was alone in a city that was two hundred times bigger than Smoky Valley. Could I have booked the first flight home and tried to change her mind? Of course. I thought about it. I even got as far as picking my phone up off the counter and searching for flights. But I didn't book anything. Instead, I just stared at the new crack in my screen and felt the crack in my heart continue to get bigger.

Eventually, the sadness and anger faded, and I pulled myself back together. I embraced my new life in San Diego, made friends, and started living again, packing my days with fulfilling experiences rather than sitting alone in my apartment.

But even after I recovered, I started to realize my heart wasn't the same as it was before. Before, my mantra was, "it's either going to work or it won't, but I won't half-ass it." So, I'd always jump into relationships with my whole heart. But that breakup affected me differently. I wasn't so free to let people in anymore. I hate to admit it, but it was almost like I was scared to get too close to someone again. That is, until I met Kasie.

I mean, damn, I was so fucking willing to part with my heart when she came into my life. The emptiness I felt, she filled it; her magnetic smile and infectious personality, her spontaneity, and her happiness… I never had a choice but to hand my heart over. But it wasn't a romantic exchange; there was just something about her that I felt deep inside, like she was someone I could trust to keep my heart safe. It was in that moment that I knew I had found a best friend in her.

"Bro?" Connor waves his hands in front of my face to bring me back to the present. "You know if I could have avoided it—"

"I know. It's all right, brother. I appreciate the heads up."

Olivia and her family are family friends, so I knew they'd get an invite. I'd be stupid to think otherwise. I just figured with all things considered, she wouldn't come.

"Don't mention it. Hey, plus," he says with

a grin, "you've got Kasie now. She's cool. I'm glad you guys took the plunge. She brings out that pretty smile of yours." He chuckles and jokingly jabs my shoulder. "Seriously, though, whether you know it or not, you've found something special, bro. You both have been glowing all day and night."

"It's just the honeymoon stage, man. Eventually, she'll drive me crazy."

"Oh, dude, she'll stress you the fuck out sometimes. But that won't matter if you love her, because you'll keep coming back for more."

"Maybe." I half shrug, trying not to sound so certain that there is no romantic future between Kasie and I.

"All right, man," he says before smacking the table gently. "Well, she's sleeping, and you look tired, so I'm going to head out." He stands up and chugs his beer.

"You sure?"

"Yeah, I need to get some sleep anyway, so I can kick your ass on the golf course tomorrow."

"Yeah, that's not going to happen, bro. I'm telling you—I'm going to be Tiger Jr."

"Sure," he drawls sarcastically.

We give each other a hug and he walks out the door.

I take a seat back at the table, rub my temples, and space out, wondering how I'll react to seeing—and who knows, maybe even speaking—to Olivia again. What do I do? Avoid her, talk to her, don't talk to her but at least smile and wave? Fuck if I know.

"Is everything—"

"Shit!" I exclaim, jumping and nearly spilling my beer all over myself when I hear Kasie's voice. "Kasie, you scared the hell out of me!"

She giggles softly, leaning against the bedroom doorway. "Damn, I know my hair's a mess, but I just woke up. Give a girl a break."

I chuckle. "Sorry, did we wake you?"

"You did, actually. *But* you can make it up to me with a shoulder rub." She looks at me like she just gave me the deal of the century. A while back, I turned into Kasie's personal massage therapist when she was sore after working out and I decided to brag about my massaging skills. I've never taken classes or anything, I just happen to be good with my hands.

"Really? It's after midnight."

She looks at me with a sulky expression and crosses her arms. "But you woke me up." Her voice is a sweet, tired rasp. How can I deny her right now?

"Man, I would be screwed if you really *were* my girlfriend."

"Why? Because you're a sucker, and you would give in even more than you already do?" She smiles happily.

"Yes, exactly. You are so spoiled."

"I can't help it that I'm cute." She shrugs, and I motion for her sit on the floor in front of me as I take a seat on the couch behind her. "Plus, I have to take advantage of this as much as I can, because someday, you may have a girlfriend who doesn't want you massaging me anymore."

I scoff. "I don't see a girlfriend in my future for a very long time. But if some girl happens to sneak inside my heart, she will have to accept you as my permanent plus one."

I start in on her shoulders.

"Are you sure about that? What if anytime-massages are one of those things that only couples can do?"

"What does that mean?"

Kasie sighs softly. "I don't know, maybe it's just buzzed thoughts ricocheting around my overactive brain. But before I fell asleep, I was in my head a little bit, thinking about what your brother said during lunch—how there are some memories only couples can make. What do you think would happen if we ran out of things to do together? Do you think we would still be best friends? Or would we drift apart?"

Her question throws me off a bit, because of all the sides she shows me, vulnerable Kasie isn't one that shows up often. I know she deals with random bouts of anxiety, panic attacks, and worry. And right now, it's the worry in her voice that is thick. I stop massaging her and decide to wrap my arms around her from behind.

I rest my chin on the top of her head and say, "Of course we would still be best friends. Our friendship isn't built on the things we get to do. It's built on the quality time we get to spend together. As long as we have each other, we will always be best friends."

"No matter what?"

"No matter what."

I lean in and give her one last comforting squeeze. When I do, she turns her face to mine and plants a kiss on my cheek. "Thank you for being such an amazing friend to me. I don't know what I would do without you."

"You won't ever have to find out." I smile and go back to rubbing her shoulders.

Once I'm finished, she stands up and looks ready to say goodnight, but the wincing look on my face silences her. I run my palm across my jaw, not ready to say what I have to say, but I see the impatience growing on her face now, so I just come out with it. "So, we might have to share the bed from here on out."

"Why?"

"When Connor came over, he saw my stuff on the couch. We almost got made on day one, Kase. My quick thinking saved us, but it was way too close of a call." She begins to protest, but I take her hand in mine and use my crooked smile to turn on the best-friend-charm. "It'll be fine, trust me. It's not like we have to do anything. Just pick a side of the bed. You keep the blanket on the bed and I'll use the extra one, and we'll sleep without a care in the world, especially knowing that we actually look like a happy couple if we get surprised again." She fiddles with the hair tie on her wrist, and I can see the wheels turning, so I make one last convincing effort. "It's just two weeks. Two weeks and everything goes back to normal. But while we're here, we have to look like a happy couple. It's too big a risk to have my stuff on the couch."

She takes a deep breath and makes a face at me like she knows I'm right and hates to admit it. "All right, fine. But if you end up pressed against me and I feel something poking me, I swear…"

I laugh and raise my hands in the air. "That's not going to happen."

At least I hope not.

Chapter Five

Kasie

~ Day 2, Monday ~

It's 8 a.m., and I'm sitting at the wrought iron table on our bedroom patio, looking out at the ocean. I've been out here for an hour now, slowly sipping my coffee. It's a little chilly this morning, so I've got my knees tucked to my chest beneath Donnie's big T-shirt. I'm trying to be patient and let Donnie sleep, but I'm starting to give way to the hunger.

Fifteen more minutes go by before my patience runs out. I head back inside and jump on Donnie's back. "Good morning, sleepyhead! Wake up, it's time for breakfast."

"What time is it?" he groans with his head buried beneath the pillow.

"Almost nine," I fudge slightly. "I'm starving. I've been up for over an hour now." I lean down closer and say, "I *would* just go eat without you, but you know, a happy couple would get up and have breakfast in paradise together, so I'm stuck waiting for you."

He flips over, and I yelp as I fall on the mattress beside him. He narrows his eyes at me. "I see what you're doing."

"I don't know what you're talking about." I sit up and smirk innocently as I toss my hair over my shoulders.

He shakes his head and finally gets out of bed.

After throwing some comfy clothes on and taming the bed head, we make our way to the outdoor café. We find our seats and order mimosas and breakfast soon after.

I look out at the beach and watch as it begins to come alive with people. Some people jogging, some setting up umbrellas and beach chairs, and others already splashing in the waves.

"So, Olivia is coming to the wedding, and most likely the bachelorette party too," Donnie announces after our mimosas arrive.

I widen my eyes. "You're kidding."

"I wish I was. That's why my brother stopped by last night, to give me a heads up."

I shove my hair back away from my face and try not to sound like a total bitch. "I swear, if she gets in your head out here and hurts you again, I will put my jiu-jitsu training on display."

Donnie smiles big and then says, "Calm down, killer. She's a family friend, so I'm sure she's just here out of respect."

"Or, she hasn't moved on, and she thinks this is the perfect time and place to rekindle the flame she snuffed out."

"Nah, that's crazy."

"Girls are crazy." I raise my glass to my lips and take a drink.

"Well, even if that *is* the case, I'm not interested in rekindling anything with her."

"Good because if you fake-cheat on me while I'm out here pretending to be your everything, we're going to have some problems."

He drops his jaw and looks offended.

"Damn, Kase, is that the kind of guy you take me for?"

"Sorry, I forgot to filter my thought before it slipped out of my mouth." I blush, because I totally sound like a jealous girlfriend right now. I'm just worried for my best friend. He's happy, and I want it stay that way. "See, girls are crazy."

"Well, you're my kind of crazy." He grins and it melts my over-protective heart. I smile back.

On the outside, he seems unbothered by the news of her coming, but for a split-second, I see his eyes glaze over like a worst-case scenario just played in his head. I give it an uncharacteristic silent minute before I press, "So, how do you feel about seeing her again? I mean, she's your first love. It's got to make you at least a little nervous."

He half-shrugs. "Yeah, but it's whatever. Anyway, how's your drink?"

I know he changed the subject to get out of talking about her, and I decide not to full-court-press him on it. There's always time for that after more alcohol.

After breakfast, we head back to our room and finish getting ready for the day. I pick out my coral, polka dot t-shirt and denim overalls. Donnie chooses a pair of army green chino joggers and a black t-shirt. He doesn't style his hair, but he's one of those lucky guys who looks handsomely rugged with messy hair.

Before we part ways, we meet up in the lobby with Donnie's parents and Connor and Mila.

Hank gives Charlotte a sweet goodbye kiss, and Connor does the same with Mila. I look at Donnie. He grabs my waist and pulls me closer, until we're chest to chest and I'm looking up into his green eyes. I don't know if it's the lighting, but his green eyes look extra green right now, and they are kind of mesmerizing. He quirks the corner of his mouth into an impish grin that is annoyingly handsome, and it compels me to bite down on the corner of my bottom lip. The anticipation of this— whatever it is—is alarmingly titillating.

What are you thinking, Donnie?

He leans in and locks his warm lips to mine. I close my eyes and assume it will be a quick goodbye kiss but gasp quietly when I feel his rough palms cup my cheeks and his tongue slip inside my mouth.

Well, that was unexpected.

My heart races as he holds my lips captive with his. I clasp my arms around his neck, giving in to him and taking in every note of his woodsy cologne. When he moves his hands to the small of my back, I try to fight away the tingling sensation between my thighs by thinking of what color I want for my nails, but it isn't helping as much as I wish it was.

This is awkwardly enticing, and I hate-like it.

He pulls me in closer and then finally releases my lips. I open my eyes and look up at him smiling at me. Somehow, he's left me speechless, which has not ever happened. That was quite a public display. I wonder if that was an attempt to dispel any doubts his brother might have about us after finding us sleeping separately last night. If so, there are certainly no doubts now.

"Go have a good time getting pampered today, baby. You deserve it," he says, his deep voice caressing my eardrums.

I press my hand to his chest and smooth the wrinkled areas of his shirt, finally finding some words. "Thank you. And you go get a par…or a bogie or birdie. Whichever one is the good one." I laugh, tucking locks of hair behind my ear, trying not to keep staring at him.

He kisses me on my warm cheek before he and the guys walk off toward the golf course.

Wow, that was…hot.

While I try to get my heart to slow down, Charlotte, Mila, and I make our way to the Enchanted Shores spa. I get a mani-pedi every month at my favorite salon in Del Mar, but getting one here in Punta Cana at a luxury resort is a whole vibe. The spa here, oh my gosh—it is elegance at its finest. In the center of the nail bar, there's a massive crystal chandelier hanging above the marble floors. The ambient music immediately relaxes my mind and body—which is nice, because Donnie's kiss stimulated and heightened my senses in all the wrong places just a moment ago.

We're greeted with smiles and taken to the nail bar to get our treatments. I choose my design and two colors; a soft yellow and a soft pink.

"Thanks for inviting me," I tell Mila.

"Girl, of course. Hell, after that fucking goodbye kiss-turned-makeout session, we may be sisters before long." She wears a devilish grin, and it makes me blush all over again.

"I don't think he'll be getting down on one knee anytime soon. Speaking of proposals, though, I'm curious, was Connor's super-sweet?"

"Umm, it depends on how you define sweet."

"Oh no."

She laughs and swipes a strand of hair away from her eyes. "He did it on the jumbotron at a Detroit Tigers' home game—they're our favorite MLB team. After, we got to meet the team, and the Tiger mascot delivered a dozen roses, a bucket of beers, and a jersey signed by all the players. I loved it. My mom, not so much. But we're a baseball couple, so it was totally us."

"That is so cool! And hey, as long as it was

sentimental to you guys, that's what matters."

"Amen," Charlotte says when she finishes picking out her services and nail colors. "My boys have always been sentimental in their own right. If you can believe it, though, of the two, Donnie was always the hopeless romantic."

"No way!" I try not to sound too surprised, but I am. He's a sweet guy and I love him, but I can't picture him as a hopeless romantic. Although, if all the passionate kisses and sweet gestures I've been receiving already are any indication of what he's like in a real relationship, I guess this free trial version of him is pretty romantic.

"Oh yeah. Back in kindergarten, he had a crush on a girl in the neighborhood. One day, after church, he had this cheesy grin because he had bought her a toy ring with the church-bucks he'd saved up—they'd get church-bucks for helping out and being good during Sunday school, which explained why I hadn't got any reports of him acting up in a while. Well, the next day, after school, he asked me to walk with him to Leila's house—that was the lucky girl. So, I did, and I waited at the edge of the driveway while he walked straight up to the front door with the confidence of the world on his shoulders, knocked, and waited until her dad answered."

"Oh my gosh. I bet that was nerve wracking."

"Leila wasn't home. She had soccer practice that day. So, he asked her dad if he'd give her the ring when she got back. And of course, her dad knew Donnie was a good kid, so he was more than happy to oblige. Donnie turned around after giving Leila's dad the ring, and you'd think that boy hit the lottery."

"Aww, because in his heart, he did. That is so adorable."

I have to say, it's refreshing to hear about this whole other side to Donnie that even I haven't really gotten to see. I feel like I'm getting to know him even better than I already do, and, I don't know, it's refreshing.

Once our manicures are finished, we move on to the pedicure station—a row of high-backed, white, tufted chairs sitting atop a marble platform with cute little circular foot baths in front of them.

A couple minutes after taking our seats, Mila turns to me and says, "So, Connor and I are having our bachelor and bachelorette party a week from this Wednesday. It's not exactly a dual party, but we'll probably meet up at one of the nightclubs or bars at some point. Consider this your official invitation."

I squeal with excitement. "Girl, how exciting! I wouldn't miss it."

"Ok, great!" She beams. "I'm going to wear white, but all the girls are wearing black dresses, so if you've got something black, wear that. If not, no big deal, you'll just have to take an extra shot." She winks.

"Don't worry. I'll make Donnie take me shopping."

"That's my girl," Mila says proudly. I watch her look down at her phone as she gets a text message. Her eyes light up. I don't ask, because I don't want to be nosy, but when she looks at me, she must notice the curiosity on my face. "My fiancé just got us all invited to some big party in the ballroom tonight!"

I drop my jaw. "Oh my gosh, that's awesome! Wait, how did he manage an invite to a party while golfing?"

"That's my future husband for you." She looks at Charlotte, who nods and smiles as if to affirm the statement. "I don't know what it is, but Connor has this charisma that attracts people and makes them want to hang out with him."

"Is that a good thing or…?"

"Well, I'm more leery of people than he is, but I'll admit it *has* gotten us into some pretty cool situations…and also some awkward ones."

"My mom was like that. She was a free spirit, always meeting new people and adventuring. That's how she met my dad. She was at a visitor and nature center purchasing a couple things for an overnight hike when she struck up conversation with the cashier—my dad—who told her she shouldn't hike the area by herself because it could be dangerous. They went back and forth until finally she told him if he was so worried about her, he should just go with her. He wasn't going to, but he said, 'her smile coerced me into it.' And I believe it; she had this smile that radiated so much joy. I've never seen anyone smile like she does."

"I have." Charlotte leans towards me and points at the smile on my face. "I've seen the pictures you post of your mother. She was a beautiful woman with a beautiful smile that she passed down to her daughter. If I had to guess, I'd say Donnie has as much of a hard time saying no to your smile as your dad did to your mother's."

"Aww." I place my hand over my heart, trying not to tear up at her sweet compliment, because I really don't want to ruin my makeup. "Thank you. That's so sweet of you to say. And yes, he does have a hard time saying no. I'm kind of spoiled." I giggle.

I loved my mom. I'm so thankful that she was all about pictures and videos when she was here. I've got a bunch of them saved to my computer. Sometimes, when my anxiety starts to get the best of me, I'll go grab a bottle of wine, sit in my apartment, and just look at pictures and watch our old family videos while having a good cry. I miss her every day. Most days, I'm okay, but it's the days like graduating from college, or knowing she won't be there when I open a bakery like I always told her I would do when I was making Play-Doh pies and cakes, that it really stings. My dad tells me all the time that she'd be so proud of who I've grown into. And I love hearing him say that, but sometimes I just wish I could hear it from her.

I love you, Mommy.

When our mani-pedis are finished, the girls and I stop in at the Beach Grill. The smoky smell coming from the kitchen makes me want to order a whole rack of ribs right away, but we're waiting for the guys to finish the last hole so we can all eat lunch together. So, for now, we order fancy cocktails and an appetizer, because Mila admits she's going to be hangry if she doesn't eat something. We finish our first round of drinks, order a second round, and get halfway through the loaded nachos before the guys show up. I stand up and Donnie greets me with a hug and a kiss.

"Your lips taste like beer," I say.

"*Yours* taste like strawberries."

"It's this drink. Look how pretty it is!" I lift my drink off the table to show him and then set it back down after a quick sip.

"It's almost as pretty as you are."

He is really laying it on thick today.

He brushes a lock of hair away from my eyes, and I get goosebumps when his deep voice hums in my ear, "I missed you. Did you have a good time?"

"I had a great time. How'd you do?" I ask as we take our seats.

"Dad kicked our asses."

"Yeah," Connor cuts in. "I don't know why you don't just try to go pro, Dad. He finished two under par."

I've never understood golf talk. Donnie's tried explaining it to me before, but I get lost in all the fancy words. Plus, when I tag along with him to go golfing, it's not because I'm trying to work on being a better golfer. I just go because I enjoy spending time with him. And I want him to know that just because his best friend is a girl, it doesn't mean we can't do things that he would normally do with his guy friends. Plus, he does the same for me when I want to go get facials or have a shopping day—which is awesome, because I make him carry all my heavy bags.

Hank grunts. "I'm flattered, son, but I'm not *that* good."

The waiter stops by, and the guys order a round of beers.

When the waiter leaves, Mila turns to Connor and asks, "Okay, so I'm dying to know. How the hell did you guys get us invited to a party tonight?"

Connor takes in a deep breath and rubs his clean-shaven chin, grinning like he got away with something he shouldn't have. "Craziest fucking story. So, the hole that we were playing on at the time has an area that runs along the seashore and drops down into the rocks and shit. Well, of course, Donnie hits a chip shot and splices it over there—so much for Tiger Jr." Connor snorts and Donnie balls up a napkin and tosses it at him. "So, we go to look for his ball, even though I told him we should just drop a new one because we'd never find it—which, we didn't by the way." He gives Donnie another look.

"Just finish the fucking story, Mister Eight-Over-Par." Donnie grins, and Connor rolls his eyes.

"Well, for once Donnie's hard-headedness

paid off, because there was this guy over there standing a few feet away from his golf cart, looking down into the rocks. Donnie and I went over to make sure he was all right. He went on and told us this story about a sentimental ball he didn't mean to use but, in his drunken state, he did, and now it was sitting down there between a couple of rocks. This guy was in no shape to go get it but he was working up the courage to until Donnie—who had a little alcohol courage himself—said, 'I'll get it.'"

"Donnie Joseph Walker!" Charlotte's voice and eyes fill with panic.

"What? I was never in any *real* danger, Mom," Donnie protests, but she doesn't look any more assured than a second ago. "I've cliff-jumped *and* rock-climbed on multiple occasions. So, this was nothing."

Oh my gosh, speaking of, cliff-jumping is one of our favorite things to do together. The first time I talked Donnie into doing it with me, he was so nervous. It was a thing of beauty. I'm half his size, and I'm over there trying to talk him into being brave. After I was sure he was ready, I grabbed his hand in mine, we took off running, and never looked back. He was so happy that I pushed him to do it, and I was happy that he trusted me.

Connor continues. "He really wasn't, mom. We were in more danger with Donnie driving the golf cart. This dude drives like we have extra lives." He laughs, and Donnie shoots him an unimpressed scowl. "But it took Donnie like three minutes to get down there and get the ball. As soon as he got back up with the ball, this guy's face was bright as the sun we were standing under. He kept thanking us and was just all-around grateful. It was actually a pretty cool moment. Anyways, he took our names down, said he's hosting a party in the ballroom tonight, and told us we're all on the guest list. And best of all, the drinks are complimentary."

"So, *Donnie* got us the invite, not you?" Mila asks.

"Well, yeah, but I kept the guy company and talked to him while Donnie got the ball, so it was a team effort." Connor chuckles.

"Are you sure it wasn't just a drunk invitation that he'll forget to honor? Because, honey, if I get all dolled up for nothing, there's a couch that your ass will be sleeping on tonight."

I chuckle nervously, hoping Connor doesn't

make a joke about finding Donnie on the couch last night.

"Pumpkin," Connor says, cupping his hand beneath Mila's chin and giving her a kiss. "Trust me, we're on that list."

We finish eating and then we all head in the direction of our rooms. Mila and Connor's room is just down the hall from ours, so we walk together. Donnie links his fingers with mine, and when we get to our doorway, he twirls me around and swoops me into his arms. Even though all of this extra attention is a little awkward at times because it's coming from my best friend, I *will* admit I'm soaking it all in: the sweet compliments, being showered with random kisses, the affection. Fake or not, it *does* make me feel special and loved. *And* it's also frustrating that my best friend—who probably feels just as awkward about all this as I do—can give me the kind of attention I want in a relationship, but the guys I actually *choose* to date *always* come up short.

I smile and link my arms around his neck as he cradles me and swipes our room key to open the door. Connor follows us inside and says, "Seven o'clock, bro. Don't be late."

I giggle to myself, because Donnie is always running late. Sometimes it's five minutes, sometimes it's thirty. The only time he's not late is if I'm with him.

"We won't be late," Donnie assures. "We'll see you guys in a bit."

Connor shuts the door, and I yelp as Donnie tosses me on the couch. "Oh, no you didn't!" I drop my jaw as he throws a smirk on his face.

He laughs and turns around to walk away.

Big mistake.

I jump off the couch onto his back and apply a chokehold that catches him off guard. "Tap out!"

"Nope." He grunts, and I tighten my grip. He grabs my upper thigh where he knows I'm ticklish and I fight the urge to crack up laughing because I can feel he's about to tap out. Another few seconds go by, and he finally gives in and taps. I sigh with relief and loosen my grip, staying on his back and leaning my chin on his sturdy shoulder.

He catches his breath and says, "Damn, you are small but mighty, you know that?"

I smile at the compliment. "Thank you." I hop off his back when he reaches the bedroom. "Okay, so I need your help deciding on which dress I should wear tonight. I have a couple dress ideas. One is a long-sleeved bodycon dress with ruched detailing—" I stop when I see the deer in headlights look. Sometimes I forget he knows as much about women's fashion lingo as I do about golf. "The dress I wore to Morgan's Christmas party."

Recognition dawns on his face. "Ohhh, the one that hangs off your shoulders and accentuates your collarbones?" He asks, fancying his voice towards the end of his sentence. "Definitely wear that one. Don't even consider a second option. That one is super sexy."

"Wow, I am so surprised you remembered the dress so easily. You know, if you were my *real* boyfriend, you'd get some serious brownie points for that."

He cocks his head to the side. "Really? For remembering a dress?"

"Yes! Because it's *not* just remembering a dress. It means you were actually present *and* paid enough attention to me that you can remember what I was wearing to a party six months ago. I mean, it's either creepy or impressive." I laugh, and he frowns at me. I gesture my head toward the middle of his jeans and then give him a look like I'd want nothing more than to feel him inside me right now. "Of course, you could still get *some* brownie points." I bite my lip and start his way.

He shifts his weight and chuckles nervously, backing up into the vanity chair behind him. "What are you talking about?"

I stop in front in of him and press my hand against the fabric of his shirt, tiptoeing my fingers from his abs to his chest. I pierce his eyes with mine and say, "You know, the way you kissed me before you went golfing, it got me thinking."

"Thinking about what?"

"How both of us haven't had sex in forever. One time wouldn't hurt, would it?" I flutter my lashes.

He visibly swallows and narrows his eyes. I can tell his heart rate has increased because I feel it in his chest. "Stop playing. You're kidding, right?"

"Do you think I am?"

He studies my eyes, and I continue holding back the smirk I've been fighting since I started trying to be enticing.

After a few more intense seconds, his lips quirk up, and it compels me to break from character. I crack up laughing and fall against him. He wraps me in a friendly hug, and I'm certain he's shaking his head in annoyance with my antics.

"You almost had me. I was sitting here thinking, 'There is no way she's serious. Last week she told me she would slap me for mentioning that.' That was good. I wonder if I need to stop kissing you so deeply, though."

"Noooo!" I whine, stepping back from his hug and giving him a sulky look. "I was joking. You can't stop now."

Wow, that sounded really needy.

He looks at me curiously, probably wondering why I don't want him to stop being "the perfect boyfriend."

I sigh and answer his questioning eyes. "I'm having fun pretending, okay? I miss having someone to do all this romantic stuff with. It's been a while. I mean, it's not just me, right? Do you miss it too, like, at all? Ugh, I just made it weird, didn't I?"

"Super weird, Kase," he says, grinning from ear to ear.

"Donnie!" I groan, crossing my arms and frowning at him.

"I'm kidding. I kind of miss it too. Although, not enough to need your wing-woman skills just yet, so don't get any ideas."

"Fine, but when we get back home, I *do* need you to be a better wingman."

"Ah, come on, I thought Jeff was cool."

"Jeff was *not* cool. Do I have to remind you how much he hated my desserts? He critiqued everything I made. Like, okay, Master Baker, I'm sorry that when I frost a cake, it looks like abstract art, but I'm still learning, and it tastes wonderful, I swear. Can you believe he had the nerve to 'forget' to bring my peach cobbler to his work party? I worked so hard on that."

"Wait, the peach cobbler that you ended up giving to me?"

"Yep."

"Damn, you didn't tell me that."

"Because at that point, it was whatever. I was annoyed about it, and it didn't matter anyway."

"Of course it did," he says sweetly, and his smile warms me up. "And you know what? I'm glad he didn't take it, because he didn't deserve it. That peach cobbler was the best I've ever tasted. And who needs pretty cakes? I like your abstract ones, they have character." He grins and I roll my eyes, unable to bury the smile that forms on my lips.

"Thank you. Now, speaking of exes—"

"No, not speaking of exes."

"Donnie, we have to."

"We really don't."

"Ugh, fine, then let me ask you a hypothetical question: if you could, would you go back and change what happened between you and Olivia?"

"Is this a trick question to try and dissect my answer so you can see if I'm fit to be around her?" He laughs and I knit my brows.

Smartass.

"Just answer the question."

He leans against the wall and shoves his hand through his hair. "Does my life stay the same if I do?"

"Umm, no. That's too easy." I giggle. "The only thing that's certain is that you'd have Olivia by your side. Everything else could be the same or it could be completely different."

Without hesitation, he answers, "Then, no. I wouldn't change a thing."

"Really?" I ask with surprise on my face, not even realizing that was the answer I was hoping for until my shoulders relax and this oddly relieving feeling flows through my veins.

"Yeah. For a long time, all I could think about was having her back in my life. But then I met you. And now, I can't imagine a world without you. So, if I have to risk losing you, count me out."

"Aww, Donnie," I say, giving him a sweet smile before wrapping my arms around his neck and pretty much strangling him with a hug. His admission warms my cheeks and awakens a bunch of little butterflies in my stomach. "That is so sweet." I stand on my tiptoes and give him a big, wet kiss on the cheek, feeling special and loved. "I don't know why you stick around, but I'm glad you do."

He scoffs and creases his brows. "What do you mean, you don't know why I stick around?"

"Oh, please, you know I'm a handful to handle. Aside from my dad, you're the only guy who's ever come into my life and not been overwhelmed by my appetite for adventure, my random panic attacks, the way I'm always playing around, or even my attitude when I get hangry. You take it all in stride, and even though I don't know how you do it because even *I'm* annoyed with myself sometimes, I'm grateful that you do."

He smiles and wraps me up in his arms. "You're worth every headache."

I gasp and push him away. "That is so mean!"

He laughs and grabs me back in his arms while I give him a frown and poke out my lips.

"I'm just messing with you," he says, looking at me sincerely. "But seriously, I love you, Kasie. You're worth every smile." He lets me go and says, "Now, let's get the vodka shots flowing before the party starts."

"Yes! I need you loose and ready to dance with me once we get there."

Chapter Six

Donnie

Once we're at the party, we mix right in and get the drinks flowing. My parents decided to have a date night instead, so it's just me, Kasie, Connor, and Mila tonight. The ballroom is decorated with a modern flair. The music is familiar, the white dance floor is packed, and circular tables are spread throughout the room, dressed in long, white tablecloths with a big, bottle of whiskey and shot cups as centerpieces—my kind of party.

"How long did it take you to get ready, pretty boy?" Connor snickers at me.

Growing up, Connor always gave me shit for keeping up with my appearance. Styling my hair, coordinating my outfits, washing my face, wearing expensive cologne; all that stuff he would say pretty boys did. I didn't care though; the girls liked it.

Before I'm able to think of a smartass comeback for Connor, Kasie squeals happily because the DJ starts playing her favorite song. She pulls me to the dance floor—followed by Connor and Mila—and starts grinding her hips on me. She loves to dance sexy, and I'm usually her dance partner because, unlike when her and her girls hit the dance floor, drunk guys don't creep up behind her when she's dancing with me. So, I'm used to having her body pressed against mine. And I'm used to her perfume trying to seduce me. But what I'm not used to is my hands itching to slide down further than the small of her back like they are right now—I always keep them above her waist. I'm also not used to her dark brown eyes staring flirtatiously into mine; her gaze right now is paralyzing.

I have to say, this fake dating role we're playing has intensified the sexual tension between us. It's always been there. We're not the type of best friends who look at each other as brother and sister. Kasie and I are attracted to each other. It's not a secret. We just choose not to act on that attraction—well, that is, until this trip. But when we get back home, she'll go back to being my gorgeous best friend who is off limits, no matter how much sexual chemistry we have.

Her hands link around my neck, and my body tingles in all the wrong places when she stands on her tiptoes to pull me down close enough to lean in and brush her lips across my neck. I feel the warmth of her breath trail upwards until she gently bites my ear. Before I can process the excitement traveling through my body, she locks her soft lips to mine with no intention of letting go. She kisses me deeply, and I'm almost certain she's trying—and succeeding—to take me by surprise again. She likes to compete, so outdoing me is something I wouldn't put past her because I know our makeout session this morning caught her off guard, but I needed to make extra sure that there weren't any doubts about us.

I'm fully expecting her tongue inside my mouth, but instead, she pulls away, releasing my lips before mine were ready to let hers go. I'm oddly disappointed. She swipes her thumb across her bottom lip and winks at me.

Damn.

I'm frozen in place with my jaw half-dropped when she asks, "Are you okay?"

I scoff and shake my head with an accusing smile. "You did that on purpose, right?"

"I don't know what you're talking about," she says with a feigned innocence in her voice.

"Riiiiight. Anyway, are you ready to get some more drinks?" I extend my hand.

"It's like you can read my mind." She grabs my hand, and I lead us towards the bar.

We stand at the bar, and after we order our drinks, I hear a gruff voice call out, "Donnie?"

I look toward the direction I heard the voice in and see the guy I helped at the golf course earlier. He's standing at a table near the bar. I tell Kasie I'll just be a minute, so she waits for our drinks while I stop over to say hello and meet his wife and some other people at his table. After a bit of small talk that takes longer than I expect, I glance toward the area where Kasie was waiting for our drinks and she's no longer there. I assume she grabbed them and is waiting somewhere nearby, so I wrap it up with the group.

After exchanging goodbyes, I turn around and scan the crowd for Kasie.

There she is.

She's standing in the middle of the bar area,

next to a high-top table that holds the drinks we ordered. She's got a bubbly smile on her face, talking to some older guy who's more interested in sneaking peaks of her ass than listening to whatever she's saying.

I don't like the way he's looking at you.

I watch her for a second, mesmerized by the passion on her face as she talks; it's infectious, and she looks so happy. She makes a quick glance across the room and catches me staring, and somehow, she lights up even brighter, which I would have guessed was next to impossible.

She gives me a look as if to ask me what I'm staring at and why I'm still standing here. I shrug, dumbfounded, because I don't know either. I start toward her, and she looks amused as she goes back to the conversation.

"Ah, nonsense, Kasie," I hear the man say as I reach them. "I've known you for five minutes and can see you're worth investing in."

"Hey, baby," I interrupt, leaning in to give Kasie a kiss on the cheek. I wrap my arm around her waist and pull her closer to me. The look on this guy's face when he realizes he isn't getting Kasie in bed tonight is priceless.

"Hey, honey. This is Charles. Charles, this is my boyfriend, Donnie. Charles was telling me about all his connections in Florida and how he could help me find a perfect spot to open up a bakery in Key West."

Wait, what?

"It's a pleasure to meet you Donnie," he says as I extend my hand to give him a firm handshake, although it doesn't look like he believes it's a pleasure to meet me—more like an inconvenience. He turns to back to Kasie. "Now, what I'm about to say next are words to the wise, and you'll do good to remember this as you think about my offer; It's not about what you know, it's about who you know, if you want to get ahead."

"Yeah, well, she's doing well for herself without a handout, man." The words fall out of my mouth coated in jealousy and possessiveness.

Wow, not sure where that word vomit came from.

"Oh, I assure you, Donnie, it's not a handout." Charles runs his hand across his short salt and pepper beard. "You know, I was in my early twenties, much like I assume you two are, when I took some huge investment risks that paid off, and I haven't lived a dollar shy of seven figures ever since." He nods like he's impressed with himself, which clearly, he is. "I'm forty-two now and have vacation homes in four states."

"Wow, that's amazing." Kasie's eyes light up as she takes a sip of her drink.

You're not actually eating this up, are you?

Charles continues, "I'm merely pointing out that all it takes is one right decision to set you up for life. Big risks come with big rewards. And I'm a venture capitalist who can spot a good investment." He all but winks at Kasie and then takes out a business card, because why wouldn't he have one ready to give out? He hands it to her and quiets his voice just loud enough for me to overhear, "Why don't you take my card and give it some thought. No pressure. It has my personal phone number and email on there. If you find that you're interested, all you have to do is call and we'll talk."

"Thank you." She smiles sweetly as Charles walks away with a smug look that I'd love to punch right off his face.

After Charles is out of earshot, Kasie turns to me and says, "Wow, you really played the jealous boyfriend part well. You even had *me* convinced."

I chuckle nervously and scratch the side of neck. "Yeah…"

She widens her eyes and drops her jaw. "Wait, were you *actually* jealous?"

She almost sounds enthused.

"What?"

"Oh my gosh, you were! You didn't think I was really falling for his bullshit, did you?"

"I don't know." I half-shrug.

"Come on, Donnie. Don't you know who your best friend is? I may be after my fairy tale, but I'm not an inexperienced, naïve little girl either. I was just playing along for the hell of it. I literally told him how much I love California and how I'm going to open up a bakery there someday, and all he could talk about was his connections and money like I'm incapable of doing this without it."

"Maybe he's looking for a sugar baby," I

scoff, still kind of annoyed at Charles.

"Oh, well, in that case," Kasie says, pretending that she's going to run after him. I give her an unimpressed stare and she laughs and hugs my neck, staring up at me as she reels in her laughter. "Are you really upset?"

I huff, and I can't help but feel a little silly now. "No, I'm not. I guess I just felt like he was trying to steal my best friend away, and I didn't like that. I'm sorry, Kase, I shouldn't have gone all psycho-fake-boyfriend on him." I look away from her because I'm kind of embarrassed now.

She cups my chin in her palm and turns my face back to her. "Hey," she says softly. "I love my life in Del Mar. You're not getting rid of me *that* easily. Even if I ever *did* move again, I would buy the biggest suitcase I could find and stuff you inside, because you'd have no choice but to come with me. Got it?"

My lips form a smile.

She's kind of sexy when she's demanding.

"Got it."

"Good, because I'm not afraid to go all

psycho-best-friend on you either." She smirks, leaning her shoulder into me.

On the way back to the dance floor, we get stopped by my brother, who promptly tells us to turn around and head back to the bar for shots with him and Mila and another group of people they met. And for the next couple hours, we lose count of the shots, cocktails, and glasses of wine. Connor and Mila start laying the affection on heavy and eventually decide to head back to their room to spend some quality time beneath the sheets. After they leave the table, I look at Kasie, and I can see it: she's smashed. I'm pretty drunk too, but functional at least.

"Hey." I wave my hand in front of her face. Her reaction is slow, but she looks at me with glazed eyes. "Do you want to get out of here too?"

"What?" she asks as she takes a long blink.

"Let's head back to the room."

"Okay… Hold on." She lowers her head. I try to stop her, because that's the last thing she needs to do, but I'm not fast enough. As soon as her forehead touches her forearms, I know she's in for a long night.

She's going to throw up. I have to get her out of here.

I give her a couple minutes and then ask, "Are you ready to go?"

"Not yet. I'm trying to feel better," she whines.

"Okay. You're good. I'm just checking. Take your time."

And she usually does when she gets to this point of drunkenness. I think the longest I've sat and waited with her to be ready to force herself to walk with me was an hour. One. Long. Hour. But it beats the alternative of trying to carry her when she's this drunk. I learned on her 21st birthday how bad of an idea *that* was. She tried telling me she'd get sicker if I picked her up, but I thought she was just being dramatic. She wasn't. I picked her up, cradled her in my arms, and started walking her to her room to tuck her in like a great best friend would do. I got about halfway there, and she lost it all over my shirt. I almost threw up, too, but somehow, I kept it together *and* I didn't even drop her, which was impressive in itself.

After a couple songs finish playing, I place

my hand on Kasie's, and I can hear her start to sniffle. "I'm sorry, Donnie. I'm like sooooo drunk right now. I...I didn't mean to get this drunk. I really didn't."

"Hey, you're okay. Don't apologize. We had a good night."

"Oh my gosh, what about your brother and Mila? I'm so selfish. They should be the ones this drunk."

"Don't worry about them. They went back to their room already. They had fun too. There's nothing to feel bad about. Okay?"

"Okay. Ugh, everything is spinning. I'm going to throw up," she slurs as she tries to lift her head but lays it right back down.

"That's not going to happen—"

"Oh my gosh, and there's all these people around. I'm going to be so embarrassed. For the rest of my time here, I'll be known as the girl who threw up all over the ballroom."

She's starting to work herself up, so I start rubbing her back to comfort her. "No, you're not going to be that girl. I'm going to get you out of here before you get sick, all right?" *Please, let me be right.* She nods softly, which probably wasn't the best move, but I'm not calling it out if she doesn't. "All right, do you trust me?"

"You know I trust you."

"Okay, I need you to put your arm around me and I'm going to help you stand up, so we can start walking to our room."

"No, Donnie. I can't move."

"I thought you said you trust me?"

"I do, but—"

"Okay, so don't think, just do. All right?"

She sighs heavily. "All right."

"Let's get up." I move our chairs out and help her stand. She is so wobbly. "You're lucky I'm strong and athletic, because you are like a baby deer right now." I chuckle.

She giggles and then stops quickly. "Don't make me laugh," she whines. The mopey look on her face is adorable.

I focus on keeping her mind off throwing up

as we make our way across the room and out of the ballroom. I make random comments about the resort and decorations we're passing until we reach the final stretch.

"Okay, we're in the hallway, almost to our room. You're doing good."

"Ugh, everything is spinning. Why did I do this to myself?"

"We had fun though, right?"

"Yes, it was fun. Too much fun."

"Well, guess what?"

"What?"

"We made it to our room."

"Oh my gosh, we're here?" The relief in her voice matches the relief in the pit of my stomach, because if she *did* throw up in that ballroom, I'd feel like the worst best friend in the world.

Once we're in the room, I walk her to the bathroom and lay a towel out on the tiled floor, so it's not so cold on her legs while she sits in front of the toilet. She lays her arms on the seat and her head on her arms, which prompts a memory of when she was really drunk and rested her head on her hands on my toilet seat for so long one night that the permanent marker 'X' on one of her hands stained her forehead.

I go grab a couple bottles of water from the minifridge and set them next to her.

"I'll be right here on the bed if you need me, okay?"

"Ok. Thank you, Donnie. I love you."

"I love you too, Kasie."

I take a seat on the bed and rake my ringers through my now messy hair. I lean back on my elbows and sigh. My eyes are heavy, and I'm tired. After a minute, I sneak a peek, and she's swaying back and forth in front of the toilet. Poor girl. I wish there was more I could do.

A couple more minutes go by, and I hear the sound I hoped I wouldn't; her gagging. I jump off the bed and nearly trip over the high heels she kicked off in front of the bathroom entrance. I crouch next to her and hold her hair back as the lemon drop martinis, vodka shots, and glasses of white wine come rushing out. I flush the toilet as soon as she stops dry heaving and then start rubbing her back in circular motions as round two and three hit the toilet.

She sniffles, dry heaving and fighting another round that seems ready to come out, but thankfully, it doesn't.

I hand her a face towel and she wipes her mouth before grabbing the bottle of water I sat next to her. She takes a couple gulps and leans her head against my shoulder as I take a seat next to her.

"Can I get you anything?"

"No." She sniffles again and wipes her eyes with her palms. "Just hold me, please."

"I got you. Come here." I spread my legs around her and wrap her in my arms, resting my chin on top of her head as I lean back against the bathroom counter.

"Donnie?"

"Yes, Kasie?"

"Thank you for always being someone I can count on. Especially when I'm feeling weak."

"Of course. You know I'll always make sure you're safe."

She yawns, turning slightly to rest her head against my shoulder. I can feel her long lashes brushing against my skin with every blink, and each time, her eyes stay shut a little longer. Another minute goes by, and she slurs softly, almost like she's talking to herself. "I know. You're one of the good ones."

I smile to myself, and no more than thirty seconds later, she's asleep, breathing deeply in my arms. I lay her down gently on the bathroom floor and grab a blanket to cover her with after propping her head up on a pillow. I take my shirt off but change into a pair of sweatpants in case I have to get up and help her in the middle of the night. I take my spot on the bed but, honestly, it feels lonely without her crazy-ass up here with me.

I set my alarm for an hour and a half earlier than I'd normally get up—6:30 a.m., which I'm dreading—but I want to order breakfast to our room because I know she's going to need fuel as soon as she wakes up. And I know her schedule; she wakes up at around 7:00 a.m. every day, whether we've been up late drinking or not. I have no clue how she does it, but she does. And unless she's hungover, which I'm certain she will be tomorrow, she's always ready to eat. How that girl stays so small is beyond me, because she loves to eat, especially when it comes to sweets. And I'm not complaining, because I usually get to be her taste tester. I swear, one day, she's going to have the busiest bakery in Del Mar, and that's not just me hyping her up. She's so talented and driven, it amazes me.

~ Day 3, Tuesday ~

When my alarm goes off at 6:30 in the morning, I fight my heavy eyes and force myself to get up out of bed. It might actually be a good thing that Kasie passed out on the bathroom floor last night, because I woke up hard and I was all over the bed tossing and turning last night. Chances are pretty good that she would have felt it, and I don't even want to know how she would have reacted. I grab the pair of sweatpants that I kicked to the floor when I got too hot last night and adjust my cock before sliding them on. I go to stand in front of the patio door for a minute, looking at the beach and ocean. The sun is still coming up over the water and it's beautiful.

"All right, let's order breakfast," I say under my breath.

I peek inside the bathroom, and Kasie is still balled up on the floor, snuggled beneath the blanket I covered her with last night. Her water bottles are lying next to her and missing the lids. I can only imagine the massive hangover she's going to have today. Unlike me, Kasie doesn't do hangovers well at all. I can usually power through mine with a protein shake, a jog, or some greasy food. But Kasie will lay in bed—or on the couch— all day, swearing she'll never drink again, until she inevitably feels better and decides that she was being theatrical and drags me out to dance and drink the night away once more.

I grab the menu from the nightstand and decide on Belgian waffles for her and a T-bone steak and eggs for me. I call down and order breakfast before instructing them to deliver the food at 7:30. It should give Kasie enough time to wake up before I start shoving food in her face that she'll say she can't eat.

I hop back in bed and sit against the headboard, watching TV and scrolling through

Instagram and TikTok until I hear Kasie groaning just a couple minutes before seven.

She sits up and turns toward me, running her fingers through her messy hair. Her makeup is smudged, her eyes are heavy, and she looks just like I thought she would. She winces and places her hand against her stomach.

"Good morning, drunkie. You look worse than you did the morning after you and Morgan decided it would be a good idea to kill a whole box of wine together."

She smacks her palm to her forehead and laughs softly. "Ugh. Don't remind me. I really hope we don't have any plans today, Donnie, because I literally just want to roll up in a blanket and hide in bed all day."

"Don't worry, we don't have anything set in stone today. We probably need a day to rejuvenate and shit anyway. Our livers would probably appreciate the break."

"Mine is begging for one."

"Are you ready to eat?" I ask. She shoots me a glare like she can't believe I have the audacity to mention food right now. "What? You *have* to eat,

Kasie. You'll feel better quicker if you do."

"I can't eat anything. I don't even want to think about food."

You are so dramatic.

I decide it's safer to think it than to say it.

"All right, we don't have to go down to the restaurant and eat breakfast."

She breathes a sigh of relief. "Thank you."

"Because I already ordered breakfast to be delivered to our room." I smirk as her expression fills with disappointment.

"Donnie!"

"I know, I know. Just trust me, though. I picked out something that should be easy on your stomach and filling enough to help soak up the alcohol. After you eat, you can curl up in bed and watch TV or listen to music or whatever it is that you want to do. But first, we soak up some vitamin D on our patio and fill our stomachs."

I can tell she wants to protest a bit more, but she probably doesn't have the energy because she gives in. "Okay, fine. I have to shower first, though.

I feel disgusting."

"Alright. Food will be here at 7:30, so you have a little time."

She grabs her things and disappears behind the bathroom door long enough for our food to arrive. I hear her blow-drying her hair as I setup our food on the patio table. It's another beautiful day outside. The sun is like a warm blanket against my shirtless chest, and the ocean breeze is the crisp, cool sheets. I can hear the waves lapping not too far from our patio, and it makes me long to be covered in salty ocean water.

Kasie steps outside looking much more alive than she did when she woke up, but I can tell she's still not among the living. Her long hair is in a high ponytail, and she's wearing a pair of super-short pajama shorts and a tank top.

"What?" she asks and I snap my eyes off her sun-kissed legs and lock my eyes to hers as she takes a seat in front of her food.

"What? What are you talking about?" I narrow my eyes.

"You were staring at my legs like there was something wrong. Do I have a bruise or something?

Did I fall?"

I scoff. "What? No. Your legs are nice. I mean, there's nothing wrong with your legs...I mean, I didn't mean it like that."

"Like what?"

"Nothing, let's just eat." I chuckle, hoping she'll let it go. I didn't realize my eyes lingered longer than normal at her legs, and now I feel a little awkward about it.

"Okay." She hides her grin as best as she can, and I can tell she wants to continue giving me grief, but I think her hangover stops her. "These waffles do look really good. And smell even better. I just hope I can stomach them."

"You've got this. Fresh strawberries and blackberries, organic syrup, soft fluffy waffles. Shit, if you don't eat them, I will." Wrong thing to say, because I see a gleam in her eyes like she just found a way out of eating. Before she can speak up, I say, "*But* you have to try them first." She pokes out her lips, and I chuckle to myself as I cut into my steak.

She powers through and finishes one of the two waffles and a couple of berries before sliding her plate to me, and I meant what I said about eating her waffles. I finish every last heavenly bite and she looks at me like she always does when I help her finish her food—like I'm the human garbage disposal. I laugh, because she's never not amazed at how much I can eat. I'm used to eating a lot, though. I've got a high metabolism and an athletic lifestyle, so I've got to keep up with all the calories I burn.

"I'm going to throw in the towel and retreat inside, Donnie. The longer I sit here, the more I can feel the queasiness coming back."

"Ok, I'll be in soon. Just lay down and get some rest. I'll be your butler today. Unless you start being too bougie." I grin, and it makes her giggle as she pushes her chair out.

"Ugh." She presses her hand against her stomach again. "Donnie! I told you, don't make me laugh." She smacks my shoulder weakly.

After a few minutes, I get a text from Connor telling me that he, Mila, Mom, and Dad are heading to the beach in thirty minutes. I let him know that Kasie is viciously hungover, so barring a miracle, we'll be hanging out in our room today.

Chapter Seven

Kasie

I've been snuggled up beneath the warm blankets and in and out of naps for most of the day. I hate wasting a day in paradise, but I guess relaxing in a cozy bed while being waited on by my best friend isn't so bad either. Although right now I'm hoping for a little privacy. A couple minutes ago, I snuck over to the bedroom door and took a peek to see what he was doing in the living room. He was on the couch with a beer in his hand, and it sounded like he was watching baseball or something.

When I realized he wasn't paying attention, I shut the door quietly and locked it. One thing I've realized over the years—when I'm hungover, sometimes I just need a little sexual healing. I don't know if there's any scientific explanation or if it's all in my head, but if I'm not feeling good it seems to help, at least for a little while. And right now, I'm willing to try anything to get some relief.

I'm lying on my back, twisted up in the blankets, listening to make sure he hasn't noticed the door is shut. I'm certain I only have a few minutes before he comes knocking, wondering if I'm doing okay or in the bathroom throwing up again. I love that he's so attentive, but right now, I hope he ignores me. I wish I didn't feel so rushed. If I was at home, in my room, I'd be able to relax and really enjoy the pleasure I'm about to feel. But I have to make do with what time I have.

I slide my hand underneath my bra and twist my nipples, imagining the hands I feel aren't my own. The first face that comes into my mind is Charlie Hunnam. I imagine my hands aren't so soft and instead rugged like I'm sure his are. After my nipples are stimulated, I slide my hand down my stomach and try to slow my breaths, worried that somehow Donnie can hear me breathing from the living room. I watch the door; suddenly afraid I didn't lock it.

Why does it seem extra quiet right now?

But the door doesn't swing open, so I sneak my fingers inside my panties and play with my clit, eyes still watching the door until the pleasure forces me to close them. I curl my toes and slip the two fingers occupying my clit deep inside me. I can feel the soft flesh, and, in my head, Charlie is pinning me down with his eyes focused on mine as he thrusts into me. He's big, although it's hard to imagine because my fingers are small, but I try anyway. My breaths are growing heavier and harder to control as I spread and curl my fingers, thrusting against my palm. I'm too loud. I'm going to get caught. I've never been caught before. Oh my gosh, why do I even care? Donnie's my best friend, not my dad. If he catches me, who cares? He must do this too.

"Oh, fuck," I whisper beneath my breath, not sure how quiet the whisper actually is. But at this point, I'm starting to care less if my quiet moans aren't so quiet, because the pleasure that I'm feeling has me on cloud nine. I bite down on my lip, trying to silence myself, but it doesn't work, and another moan rasps out.

Whatever. Just keep going.

I increase the speed and intensity of my fingers as I thrust harder against my palm, feeling the tingling in my thighs. I imagine digging my nails into Charlie's back as he shoves himself deeper, over and over, pounding me until I want to scream. And then the stupidest thing in the world happens: Charlie's face transforms into Donnie's, and the gorgeous eyes that were staring at me are now the eyes that I've stared into over a thousand times. The eyes that can make me smile for no reason at all. The ones that have never looked at me with anything but love, even after dealing with my panic attacks. The same eyes that stared deep into mine yesterday morning before I was given a deep, passionate kiss that I shouldn't even be thinking about right now.

"Kasie?" I hear Donnie's voice and my eyes shoot open, not trusting the door that I supposedly locked. *Shit. Not yet. Ignore him.* I keep going, fighting the images I don't want with the ones I do, eyeing the door as I try to finish. I'm so wet right now, and I'm nearly there. "Are you okay?"

Ugh.

"I'm fine," I call out, short of breath, and I'm sure he can hear what I'm doing.

I have to hurry up.

My eyes roll back, and I sink my teeth into my lip so hard that I'm certain I'll taste blood. My entire body tingles, and my heart is racing. The anxiety of getting caught has somehow made me hotter than ever, and finally, finally—I hit my peak, my back arching and my toes curling so tightly I'm afraid my foot will cramp. After a few moments of suspended animation, I slump back on the bed for a minute, catching my breath and staring at the ceiling.

Finally, I can relax. Although, it would be nice to understand why and how Donnie snuck into my thoughts. I hope that never happens again.

I get out of bed, wash my hands, and change my panties before opening the bedroom door.

Shit.

My eyes widen. Mila and Connor are sitting on the couch next to Donnie, and I don't know how long they've been here. *Oh my gosh, I'm so embarrassed. What if they heard me?*

Try to act normal.

"Hey guys," I say, leaning against the bedroom doorframe, hoping my nervous smile doesn't give me away. Why is it when you've done something you don't want anyone to know about, you feel like it's written all over your face? How would they know? Of course they don't, I tell myself.

"Hey, girl," Mila says. "How are you feeling? You look flushed."

I chuckle, and it comes out as nervous as the smile I'm wearing. I walk toward the kitchen table to take a seat at one of the chairs, but Mila and Connor get up and insist I sit next to Donnie on the couch. I feel bad having them give up their seat for me, but they're persistent, and while my hangover isn't as oppressive as it was earlier, it's still hanging around enough that I do as they say and join Donnie on the couch. I snuggle in his arms and try to forget that he was in my bedroom thoughts, but I feel kind of dirty, like I'm keeping a secret from him. I'll have to deal with it, because I am *not* telling him about that.

Mila and Connor take a seat on the floor and face us, and I answer her question. "Girl, I am definitely regretting all those drinks. Why did we do that?"

Mila laughs and Connor says, "You know the best way to cure a hangover, right?"

"Here we go." Mila rolls her eyes.

He looks at Mila with a wounded expression

on his face. "What? It's true." He shakes his head and then looks at me. "You've got to drink some more. That's what I taught Donnie back in the day when he had his first hangover. And was I right, bro?"

"You were," Donnie says. "*But*—"

"Oh, shit, not you too, man."

Donnie chuckles. "No, I mean, it's not a bad strategy. But have any of you ever tried going for an outdoor jog to kill the hangover? That's where it's at."

Everyone groans, because no one but Donnie's crazy-athletic ass wants to go for a jog when they're hungover. I remember the first time we were hungover together: I was over there dying and he's like 'I'm going for a run, want to come?' I thought he was joking, but nope, he was dead serious. And so was I when I told him I'd rather just go ahead and die.

"What you really need is this." Mila digs in her backpack purse and pulls out a tea packet. "It's ginger tea, and I'm telling you, it will make you feel better. I also have some ginger gummies."

"Don't mind my fiancée, she's one of those

superfood buffs."

Mila smacks Connor's arm. "Hey, when you've got the man-flu, don't act like you're not begging me to make some fresh ginger and lemongrass tea." She turns her attention back to me. "Anyway—without any extra comments from the peanut gallery—peppermint and lavender essential oils always help with the nausea, too. I've got some, if you want to try them?"

"No offense, guys, but Mila's got the only method that sounds appealing right now. I'm down, girl."

Half an hour goes by before the combination of ginger tea, essential oils, and sexual healing work whatever magic each possess. Everyone is lounging in our infinity pool, so I get changed into a cute pink bikini and step outside.

"She's alive!" Connor hollers, with his hands in the air.

"Damn, girl, can I holler?" Mila lowers her sunglasses, looking me up and down.

I giggle and plaster a big, cheesy smile on my face. "Y'all are going to make me blush." I walk over to Donnie, who's seated on the edge of the pool with his feet dangling into the water. "Can you help me with my suntan lotion?"

"I'd do anything for you, sexy." He grins, and I roll my eyes.

"You are too much."

"How are you feeling?" Mila asks, as Donnie starts rubbing the lotion on my back and shoulders.

"Oh my gosh. I'll put it this way, I don't feel like I'm going to die anymore. I owe you so hard, girl."

"Trust me, just having you out here is payment enough," she says before taking a sip of her mixed drink.

"Damn, what's that supposed to mean?" Donnie asks from behind me as he finishes the small of my back and goes lower to get my legs.

"Oh," I gasp softly, as my eyes widen in surprise, because I figured he'd just stop at my back. I try to ignore the awkward, tingling sensation I feel when his hands rub the lotion into my upper thighs—I think I might still be a little horny. My heart races a bit, and I give myself a stern talking to about just relaxing and remembering that the hands that are rubbing me right now are my best friend's.

"I said what I said." Mila giggles.

Once Donnie finishes my legs, I turn around and narrow my eyes, trying to see if he purposely meant to tease me.

"Sorry, I was in the zone," he whispers. "I didn't mean to, uh, get so close to, uh, you know, your—"

"Uh-huh," I say, hoping I've transferred all the awkwardness I felt over to him. I grab the lotion and apply it to my stomach and chest and then step down into the pool. The water is colder than I expect it to be, but it feels good because it's got to be at least ninety-five degrees out here.

I join Mila and lean my forearms on the edge of the pool, looking out towards the beach full of people. "Girl, you have that pre-wedding glow. I love it. How are you doing with everything, though?"

Mila takes a deep breath. "Umm, excited, anxious, and everything in between." She sighs. "I just want everything to be perfect."

"It will be. Just don't sweat the small stuff and soak in every moment."

"Solid advice."

"And easier said than done, I know," I say, chuckling. "So, do you have a lot of family coming in for the wedding?"

"Umm, my parents, my sisters, and then a handful of other family members coming in from Laos, which is where the majority of my family still lives."

"Oh, are you originally from Laos, too?"

"No, I've visited a few times, but I was born and raised in Michigan. Sometimes I wish my parents would have emigrated to a state where the warm months outnumbered the cold ones, but I do love the beautiful nature scenery in Michigan. We don't go much, but there are some unforgettable hiking trails."

"We should go hiking one of these days. Donnie and I can come up and we'll rent a cabin and make a weekend out of it."

Her eyes light up. "Absolutely." She looks over at Connor across the pool and hollers, "Hey, honey, we're going hiking with Kasie and Donnie sometime this year. Okay?"

"Sounds good to me," Connor says with a thumbs-up as he and Donnie continue their conversation.

"Happy wife, happy life. He gets it." Mila laughs. "So, now that the guys are out of earshot, I have to know. What is it like dating your best friend?"

"Honestly, not as awkward as I thought it would be. But we've never been the 'brother-sister' type of best friends."

"What kind of best friends were you then? Best friends with benefits?" She chuckles.

I gasp and widen my eyes. "You are so dirty! No, we weren't best friends with benefits. We've just always been playful with each other, you know? We've got this sexual chemistry that we ignored for so long, and eventually it just kind of boiled over until we couldn't deny it anymore." I glance over at Donnie, who's lowering himself back down into the pool with a beer for himself and Connor. He catches me staring and grins, which for whatever reason compels me to bite down on the corner of my bottom lip.

Ugh, what am I doing? Why am I so horny right now, and why is my best friend suddenly tempting to me?

"So, it wasn't actually his smile that did you in?"

"I didn't say that," I say dryly, turning my attention back to Mila.

"Oh, you didn't have to. That look said it all." She gives me a wicked smirk. "So, what was it? You saw him naked, didn't you? Please tell me you walked in on him coming out of the shower or something like some cheesy rom-com."

I giggle. "Okay, that does not actually happen in real life."

"Umm, think again. During my sophomore year in high school, I walked in on Connor—and a few other guys—changing in the locker room."

"Oh. My. Gosh. You're kidding!"

"Nope, that's the honest truth. I was trying to avoid someone in the hallway and just dipped inside the first door I saw, and it happened to be the boy's locker room. Connor was standing there, completely naked, and I just froze. The other guys freaked and covered up, but he just stood there, completely unfazed, and kept doing his thing. I'm sure I was beet red, but damn, girl, when I tell you my life was changed when I saw what I saw."

I crack up laughing. "That is literally the best story ever. I'm still sticking with my story, though. I'm a hopeless romantic, like Donnie. I guess it was only a matter of time before our hearts lined up together."

"Damn," she says disappointedly. "I was really hoping for a juicy story."

Even though I haven't seen Donnie naked, I will admit that I *have* seen the outline of his cock beneath his boxer-briefs. The very first time I saw it, my heart pulsed against my ribcage. It was totally innocent, though. He walked out of his bedroom in his boxers and laid a couple outfits on the couch for me to help him choose from. I hadn't realized our friendship moved to the see-each-other-in-our-underwear stage, which is a sacred step, to be so comfortable around someone that you can let them see parts of you that not everyone gets to see. I didn't want to make him feel weird for trusting my eyes and my thoughts, but it was so spontaneous that I'm pretty sure he noticed how awkward I was. I got all fidgety and didn't want to seem like I was staring at the V lines that dipped either side of his hips or his shirtless chest, so my eyes went to the only clothed area, and that's when I saw the outline—a *big* outline. I remember my heart was racing, I was talking a million-miles-a-minute, and my mouth started to get dry; I was a wreck

Hmm, I wonder how he felt the first time he saw me in just a bra and panties?

A silent minute passes before Mila turns to me and asks, "Have you guys said the L word yet?"

"Love? No."

She moves closer and whispers, "I think he's in love with you."

I widen my eyes and choke on the air. I don't think the plan is for anyone to actually think we are in love. Infatuation from the honeymoon stage, yes, but not in love. I try to cast a little doubt without sounding like I don't want him to be in love with me. "Girl, you're talking about the guy who not long ago had sworn off relationships altogether. I'm pretty sure love is the furthest thing from his mind."

"And I'm talking to the girl who changed his stubborn mind. He may have enjoyed the single life, but he's always been a lover-boy, so it was just a matter of time."

I shrug and change the subject, "Speaking of relationships, he told me his ex is coming. Should I be worried?"

I hate to sound like a jealous, insecure girlfriend, but I'm curious to see what Mila's take on Olivia being here is. Especially since my best friend doesn't want to talk about it.

Mila squeezes her eyes shut and crinkles her nose. "So, it might be my fault that she decided to come."

"Why *your* fault?"

Mila sighs. "She's my best friend Penelope's younger sister. Last week, I was having drinks at Penelope's house, and Olivia was there when Connor texted me and told me that you and

Donnie had started dating. And I may have drunkenly bragged about it—okay, I definitely bragged about it. It was a petty move, I know, but since she wasn't going to come to the wedding, I just wanted to make sure Olivia heard that Donnie was doing just fine without her."

"Oh. I mean, it could be a coincidence, right?"

Come on, Kasie. You're not that naïve.

Mila squints. "Girl, no, I don't think so. I'll be honest, she's a sweet girl, but she never really moved on from him, and even sweet girls look out for number one. He was her first love, just like she was his. So just be careful around her and don't let her get in your head or make you question anything."

My stomach twists, and I look over at my best friend, who's smiling, not a care in the world, probably not even realizing that his heart could be in danger. I'm worried. If she wants him back, she could screw with his head, and he's in such a great headspace now. I can't let that happen. No, I *won't* let that happen.

I must be silent for too long because Mila

interrupts my thoughts and says, "I swear I'm not telling you this to scare you. Donnie is loyal and faithful and *for you*. I mean, the guy literally has stars in his eyes when you're around. Just the way he looks at you today versus the way he looked at you a couple days ago…it's different. Trust me, he's falling, and hard. Even if he doesn't know it yet."

I smile softly and then look at Donnie across the way, and he must feel me staring, because he looks up and pierces my gaze with his green eyes. He cracks another smile, and it sends my heart racing.

You're not really falling for me, are you? No, we talked about this. Everything we're doing is fake. Everything we're feeling is fake.

After a while, everyone's stomachs begin to rumble. Mila and Connor head off to enjoy a dinner date, and I suggest Donnie and I eat in our room.

Partly because I want to talk to him about what Mila told me, and partly because I still don't have the energy to get all dolled up. We say our goodbyes, and Donnie and I get changed into comfy clothes, order our dinner, and set up everything on the dining table once it arrives.

Donnie pulls my chair out, and since no one is around to see him do it, it surprises me *and* makes me think about Mila's comment about him falling for me. I'm trying not to, because I really am enjoying the special treatment. But I need to make sure we're still on the same page.

"Thank you," I say, taking my seat and watching him take his across from me. I begin cutting my chicken. "So, umm, your food looks good."

"Yeah, yours does too," he says. I don't look up, but I can feel his eyes burning a hole into my lowered head. "Okay, what's up?"

"What's up? What do you mean?" I ask, acting like I don't know that my best friend can read me like a book. It's just another thing I admire about him. He notices when I'm acting differently. It doesn't matter if it's because I'm hangry, tired, on my period, or just overall annoyed with something;

he knows.

"Something is bothering you."

I sigh and wrap my lips around the straw to my coconut juice. I was supposed to bring up Olivia first, but I can't seem to steer my mind in that direction. "It's just something Mila said in the pool earlier."

"What'd she say?"

"She thinks you're falling in love with me."

"Oh."

"Oh? Oh, as in, you are? Or?"

He laughs a little too hard, and suddenly I'm slightly offended and relieved at the same time. It's an odd feeling.

"Of course she thinks I'm falling in love. You said Oscar-worthy performances, didn't you? What, you didn't actually believe her, did you?"

"No. I mean, I don't know. She was convincing, okay? I just got worried that the lines might be getting crossed. I know we've been playing around and teasing each other more than normal, so I just wanted to check in and make sure."

He stares gently into my eyes. "No, the lines are not getting crossed, okay? We're good. Just friends."

I nod. "Okay." *Don't mention the laugh. Don't mention the laugh. Ugh, whatever, I'm mentioning it.* "You know, you didn't have to laugh so hard at the thought of falling in love with me, though." I cross my arms against my chest.

"Wait, so you were worried that I *was* falling for you. And now you're giving me shit for *not* falling for you?" He chuckles. "Man, you're right, girls are crazy," he says, placing his palm against his forehead. I giggle, and he continues, "Seriously though, I didn't mean to laugh so hard about it. Any man would be lucky to fall for you, Kasie."

"Are you just saying that to get out of the doghouse?" I frown.

"No, I mean it."

"Really? Okay, think quick. If you mean it, say something sweet about my eyes."

"Your eyes? Girl, they're so beautiful and bright, I bet the stars get jealous." He smirks, and I roll my eyes, smiling from ear to ear.

"You are so cheesy. I love it." I take a bite of my food and swallow the relief I now feel. "Soooo, don't kill me, but there *is* something else." I watch his face go from smiling to exaggerated annoyance as he groans. "What? We *have* to talk about the elephant in the room named Olivia. You know I wouldn't push you to if we weren't about to see her, but I feel like I need to know where your head is at. I'm worried for you. I don't want you being vulnerable around the girl who made you stop believing in love. I mean, look at me. Why do you think my dad always comes to visit me in California instead of me going back home?"

"Because you'd get arrested for kicking your ex-boyfriend's ass?"

I chuckle softly. "No… Because I'm afraid if I run into him, I'm going to have a massive panic attack that I won't be able to pull myself out of, and if that happens, then he won't be able to see that the fragile, eighteen-year-old girl he took advantage of turned into a strong, put-together, badass woman."

"Do you think he's still the same douchebag he was all those years ago?"

"Oh yeah. He lives down the street from my dad now, and my dad confirmed that he's still an ass. It just makes me so mad because…ugh, never mind, we're supposed to be talking about you, not me."

"No, go on. Don't hold back."

"I want to go back home," I say desperately. "I miss it. I don't know why, but lately it's hitting me harder that I haven't been back in so long. I feel like I want to go and visit and see everything and not feel so fucking nervous to be there. I hate that Greg took my home from me, and I hate even more that I let him."

"You didn't let him."

"By staying away, I did. I'm proud of who I am now, and I don't just want *him* to know it, I want *everyone* who looked at me like I was a promiscuous slut who got what she deserved back then to see that their disapproval may have broken me initially, but eventually it pushed me to become the best version of myself."

"Hell yeah, it did. You're what, a year away from opening up your bakery?"

"Well, I start the certificate program in August, and once I get through that, I just have to find a vacant space and start drawing up designs and stuff. I'm not really sure how long it'll take, but I hope within a couple years, I'll be open for business. Anyway, I'm sorry that I'm being kind of a hypocrite, saying you should confront your past when I haven't really dealt with mine yet."

"Nah, you're good, Kasie. I get where you're coming from. And I'd be lying if I said I wasn't nervous about seeing her after all these years, because I really don't know how I'll feel until I do. But hey, I'm not alone."

"Yeah, you have a hot, fake-girlfriend to flaunt on your arms." I giggle, placing my chin in palm like I'm a prize.

"Well, yeah, but that's not what I meant," he says. I cock my head to the side as he continues, "What I meant is, no matter what happens, I know I have you to lean on if things go south. And that's a kind of comfort that I can't even put into words. Because of you, I know I'll be okay."

Awww.

My heart flutters, and I catch my breath staring at his smile.

After dinner, we decide on a cozy night in, binge-watching movies together. Before I know it, it's ten o'clock, Donnie's asleep, and I'm stuck in his arms—we left the patio door open earlier to let the nice breeze in, but when I started to shiver as it got colder, he pulled me into his arms. He's been holding me ever since, and I'm completely okay with it. If I'm being honest, though, it scares me that I am, because I should know better than to be getting used to this. It's dangerous; his heart is not available, and it's like mine is just begging to be broken.

And even though I'm enjoying this danger of being held against his warm body, I'm wide awake now and need to burn off some energy, which is kind of perfect, because a late-night walk on the beach is an excellent excuse to get away and collect myself.

I try wriggling out of his arms, hoping he'll feel me moving and just turn over, but his arms clamp me in tighter.

"Ugh, why do you have to be so strong?" I mutter beneath my breath, slowly lifting his arm off me before I breathe in the sexy timber and sandalwood scent from his deodorant that follows his arm.

Once I'm free, I go to slide off the bed.

"Hey, are you okay?" I hear him mumble, his voice tired and gruff.

"Yeah, I'm fine," I answer, turning to look at him. He can barely open his eyes, they're so heavy. "I'm just going to go for a walk on the beach. I need to burn off some energy, or I'll be up all night."

"Do you want me to come with you?"

"That's sweet, but no. Just get some sleep. You've had a long day taking care of me."

"All right, be careful."

"Okay. Don't worry, it's safe out here." I finish sliding off the bed and go to grab my oversized hoodie and joggers for my walk.

It's beautiful out tonight. The light from the moon is reflecting off the calm, dark ocean, the evening breeze is cool but not too cold, and the beach is all mine—for the most part. I feel right at home as I walk alongside the water, taking in the scenery around Punta Cana. I bet in the daylight this area is beautiful and hopping with people and entertainment. But tonight, it's still and peaceful. After a bit, I find a spot to sit in the cool, soft sand and just stare out at the stars in the sky, breathing softly, and taking everything in.

After a few minutes alone, a soft voice from behind me asks, "You can't sleep either?"

I look over my shoulder and smile when I see Charlotte walking up. I wave and pull my sleeves up over my palms and hug my knees to my chest as she takes a seat next to me. "Unfortunately, not," I say. "I've been recovering from a massive hangover all day and now that I have, I've got more energy than I know what to do with. Donnie's been a total sweetheart, taking care of me all day, so he's passed out already. What's keeping *you* awake?"

"Oh, sweetie, by this point, not sleeping is just a part of life for me. You know, when you have kids, they don't tell you that you'll never sleep peacefully again, even when they're all grown up and out of the house." She laughs gently. "Sometimes, I think I sleep less now than I did when they were newborns."

"Aww," I say with a giggle. "My dad says the same thing. You should have seen him when I moved to California the summer after I graduated high school. He was so nervous, probably more nervous than I was, and that's saying something."

"Forgive me if I'm prying, but why the big move?"

"My boyfriend at the time, he posted a humiliating video starring yours truly on Instagram, and basically the whole town saw me giving out lap dances like they were candy. It was stupid, but I was young, drunk, and on top of that, I had tried smoking weed for the first time in my life, so I was not in my right mind at all. He was supposed to protect me if things went downhill, because I was already super nervous about smoking, but instead, he recorded me and was in the background laughing the whole time. The fact that I wasn't taken advantage of that night is a miracle."

"That's terrible," Charlotte says, knitting her thin brows.

I brush a few strands of hair away from my face. "Yeah. I felt like the whole town turned against me. The girl I am today would have reacted a lot differently. But at barely eighteen years old, I believed everyone had to love me all the time, so when they didn't, I couldn't handle it. I'm just glad that now I know the only person who needs to love me all the time is me."

"Well, let me tell you something, you are wise beyond your years to have figured that out already. I know I didn't know you back then, but I admire who you are today, especially because of who my son is today. I know that is in part due to you."

"I don't know about all that, but thank you." I smile, feeling humbled by her faith in me.

"It's true," she says, nudging my elbow. "You know, of my two sons, Donnie was always the one I didn't have to worry about, until I did. And boy did I worry about his future. Now, don't get me wrong, there is no problem with finding yourself and being a bachelor for some time. But the second he told me that he didn't believe in love anymore; I heard it in his voice and it broke my heart because that is not my Donnie. But about a year ago—even before I officially met you at Coach Henry's funeral—I stopped worrying so much about his future. Do you know why?"

"Why?" I ask, curious for her answer.

"Because of you. There was this night, it was kind of late, but I had FaceTimed him just to check up and see how things were going before heading off to bed. When he answered the phone, he was driving—which I wasn't too thrilled about, because he knows better than to answer the phone while driving—and I could tell he was speeding, too—again, not thrilled." She grins, and I giggle as she continues. "But he said, 'Mom, I can't talk right now. I'm on the way to meet Kasie. She just had a panic attack and is pulled off to the side of the road, alone. I don't know what to do, but I don't want her to be by herself.' It was in that moment that I knew love was still in his heart."

"I remember that night. I remember being so scared that he'd look at me like damaged goods and end our friendship, because I hadn't told him about my anxiety and panic attacks. But he wasn't bothered at all when I told him. Instead, he sat there in my passenger seat, and we just talked about it and his struggles and…everything. Before I knew it, we had been sitting there for so long that a police officer stopped by to check on us." I chuckle softly, and suddenly this aching, longing feeling breaks into my heart and makes me wish I was back in our hotel room, stuck in his arms again. "He makes me feel like I'm the only girl in the world. You've raised a great man."

Charlotte smiles. "He sure adores you, Kasie. Now, I'm not trying to butter you up, but do you know what's even more comforting to me? It's the way *you* look at *him*. When he talks, your pretty brown eyes light up, and you hang on every word he has to say. I want you to know how much I appreciate you being there for my son when I couldn't be."

Aww, I could cry right now.

That is literally the sweetest thing ever, and now I feel like such a shitty person because she's going to be absolutely heartbroken when she hears of our "breakup." Suddenly this fake relationship idea doesn't seem so innocent. In a perfect world, I would confess right now and beg her not to hate me for being deceitful. But I gave Donnie my word, and that's something my dad taught me never to go back on. So, whether I feel like shit or not, the show must go on.

I wiggle my toes in the sand and a smile splits my face. "Well, I see where he gets his ability to make me smile from ear to ear. Thank you, you are so sweet."

We talk for a little while longer before Charlotte decides to head back to the resort.

I sigh to myself and look up at the twinkling sky. "What am I doing, Mom?" I ask under my breath. "I'm in over my head, aren't I? Lying to people who care about me, having these weird, unexplainable feelings for Donnie that show up out of nowhere, me thinking that he's getting lines crossed when maybe it's me. Am I the one who's somehow forgetting this is all just an act? This isn't going to end well, is it, Mom?"

Chapter Eight

Donnie

~ Day 4, Wednesday ~

I wake up to the earthquake that is Kasie jumping on the bed so close to me that if I roll over, I'm certain she will tumble on top of me.

"Wake up, honey bun! The sun is bright, the sky is pretty, and I stepped outside earlier—the temperature is perfect."

"Perfect for what?" I groan. "And what time is it anyways?"

"It's 8:30 in the morning. I let you sleep an extra thirty minutes before being annoying." She giggles, and as much as I want to protest, I'm glad she's back to normal.

I must be crazy to have missed being woken up like this.

She jumps off the bed, and I turn over to see

her dressed in daisy dukes and a pink bikini top. Her long hair is draped over her shoulders, and she's got a sweet smile on her face. "Since you were a perfect gentleman, taking care of me yesterday, I decided to treat you to breakfast on the beach," she says. "Come on, I've got the towels packed, sunglasses, extra sunscreen, your swim shorts laid out, and I even had room service deliver our food in to-go boxes earlier, so everything is ready. Let's go, get up." She grabs hold of my arm and struggles to pull me up.

"You know, I've never met anyone who wakes up happier than you do."

"I'll take that as a compliment," she says with a cute quirk of her lips.

I finally get up and around and we're off, walking arm-in-arm to find a spot on the beach together. Something feels different about the way her arms are wrapped around mine this morning; it's closer and sweeter. Whatever it is, I kind of like it. I miss doing little things like this in a real relationship.

"There," Kasie says, interrupting my thoughts and pointing out an open spot in the sugary sand.

I set her packed beach bag down in the sand and lay our towels out. When she sets our food down on each towel and we take our seats, she pours mimosas and hands one to me.

I look at her and raise a brow, impressed. "You just thought of everything, didn't you?" She smiles proudly as I take a gulp. "So, how was your walk last night?"

"It was good. I actually ran into your mom, and we sat and talked for a bit."

"Oh yeah? What did you talk about?"

"You."

"Really?"

"Yep. Donnie, her heart is going to be so broken when we break up. What are we going to do?"

"Stay together," I say, matter-of-factly, and it makes her choke on her drink. I laugh and lean away as she smacks my arm.

"Oh my gosh, you weirdo. Look what you made me do." She points to her chest, where a few mimosa drips are sliding down between her boobs and past the string of her bikini top.

It prompts a flashback of the first time she told me to stare at her chest—like *really* stare.

'I have nice boobs, right?' she asked as she came out of the dressing room in a dress that hugged her petite frame. 'I mean, they're not big, but would you say they're nice and perky?'

It was such a random question that it threw me off, but after I got ahold of myself, I felt honored, like I'd just been accepted into some secret club or something. Here I was, a guy—her best friend, yes, but still a guy—and she's comfortable enough to ask me to stare at her body and answer a pretty personal question. I was nervous as fuck that I'd say the wrong thing and she'd build a wall to remind herself not to go there with me ever again. Fortunately, I must have given the right answer, because she plastered a cheery smile on her face, turned around, and went back to trying on clothes as I breathed a sigh of relief that my answer didn't come out pervy.

As I watch the drips trail down to her toned stomach, she says, "Wipe them off."

"What?"

"Wipe my drink off my chest and stomach." Her tone is mischievous, and so is her smile.

"No."

"You better hurry, you know where the drips are heading after my stomach, and I don't know about you, but I'd rather not reach third base out here in front of all these people."

"You're not serious." Except, I see the competitive look in her eyes. She doesn't think I'll do it, so maybe I'll turn the tables and take her by surprise. "All right, fine. Set your drink down first."

"Okay?" She looks at me suspiciously as she sets it down.

"Where's your phone?"

"Right next to me. Why?" she asks as I glance between her and the ocean. Her eyes widen in panic and her jaw drops. "You wouldn't!"

"Wouldn't I?" I grin, standing up and scooping her into my arms.

"Donnie, don't you dare." But her command falls on deaf ears. I take off towards the ocean and she squeals, wrapping her arms tight around my neck. "Donnie!" she screams before I jump into the salty ocean water, soaking both of us.

When she comes up out of the water and flips her wet hair back, she's got this big, happy smile that brings out the sparkle in her eyes. She's cracking up with laughter and the happiness surrounding her right now shoots this warm unidentified feeling into my chest. I don't know what's happening, but I've lost all ability to form words. So, I just smile and gaze at the beautiful girl I call my best friend, lost in this moment that's sure to be a sweet memory we'll reminisce about one day.

I snap out of my trance when she jumps toward me and dunks me under the water, but when I come back up above the waves, I'm struck again. I can see my chest rise and fall, but I don't feel myself breathing. When she reels in her laughter, she replaces it with a quiet, innocent gaze, almost like whatever I'm feeling, maybe she's feeling it too. We hold each other's gaze, silent now as the waves push us gently from side to side. My stomach somersaults, and I realize that for the first time in our entire friendship, I'm nervous in her presence. Everything in me wants to grab her and kiss her. I know I shouldn't, but right now, it feels like the right thing to do.

What's going on? Did I screw myself with that "stay together" comment? I was just kidding around, heart. I didn't mean it. Break free. Look away from her.

But I don't. Instead, I swim deeper into her eyes, hoping she won't let me drown.

There's no going back, I lie to myself, hoping it'll give me the courage to just kiss her and see what happens.

But then reason kicks in. *Of course, I can go back. I haven't kissed her yet. It's only in my thoughts. She'll never even know I thought it.*

She tucks her hair behind her ears, looking up at me closer now and blinking sweetly as she quirks up a corner of her soft lips. It's like she's daring me to kiss her, and it's driving me wild.

Fuck reasoning, just kiss her!

No—

Too late. Without another thought, I caress her cheeks between my palms and our lips crash together, like we know we'll never get this chance again. She presses her palms against my face, her breath heavy against mine, our tongues warring. With every smack of our lips, she's doing me in. I don't want this kiss to end, but the ocean has other plans because it sends a strong wave to slam against us and push us apart.

"I'm sorry," she says quickly, and I'm not sure why, because I'm pretty sure I initiated that kiss.

"No, I'm sorry. That was—"

"A heat of the moment thing."

"Yeah, exactly. It didn't mean anything."

"Right. And it's your fault anyway," she says plainly.

I widen my eyes and exclaim, "My fault? What? Why?"

"It turned sexual when you made me choke on my drink and spill it on myself."

"Umm, no, you were the one who turned it sexual, talking about reaching third base out here and shit. What is wrong with you?" I chuckle and she gasps, smacking my arm.

"Hey, these last few days have intensified the sexual tension between us, I can't help it if I'm extra horny because of it."

"Wow—"

"What? You're not?" She crosses her arms and looks at me like she already knows the answer but wants to hear it from me.

"I am, I just didn't…"

"Expect to admit it?" she asks, and I nod, still stunned and curious about where this conversation is headed, because this is uncharted territory. I feel like an explorer who just found new land, and I don't know what to do with it. "I didn't either. Does it make you feel awkward?"

I take a deep breath and scratch the side of my neck. "Honestly, I feel like it should, but it doesn't. I mean, we know we're attracted to each other, that's not a new revelation, so…" I pause, watching the way the wind plays with her hair. "You know what? I'm just going to say it; I like kissing you, Kasie."

She looks down at the water and then back up at me. "I like kissing you too. But no more kissing when no one's around, agreed?"

"Yeah, agreed."

"And I mean, we can enjoy kissing each other without changing us, right?"

"Of course."

"Ok, good. Now, let's go eat our food before the seagulls do."

I finish fixing my hair and step out from the bathroom, adjusting my tie one last time, and stop dead in my tracks. I swear I don't mean to, but my eyes look Kasie up and down, admiring the way her sparkly black dress hugs her frame. My jaw may as well be an anchor, the way it drops.

"Wow," I say when I recover my dignity. Kasie spins around and smiles happily as she faces me. "You are so beautiful."

Her cheeks turn pink, and her smile grows. "Thank you," she says, as she plays with the end of one of her curls. "You didn't want to save the sweet compliments for when everyone is around to hear it tonight, though?"

I shake my head. "No. That one was just for you."

"Aww, come here." She walks towards me with open arms, squeezes me tight, and leans on her tiptoes, giving me a bunch of little kisses on the cheek. I try leaning away, laughing, as she does her best to keep me close. "Come back here, I want kisses."

"Come on, don't make this weird."

"It's only weird if you make it weird." She giggles and gives me one final peck on the cheek before letting me go, and soon after, we're off toward the fancy Tex-Mex restaurant to have dinner with my family.

After a thirty-minute wait, we get seated

around our table at the back of the restaurant, and I am ready to devour some enchiladas and wash them down with the fish-bowl margaritas that the tequila-tasting lady recommended to us.

When our waitress brings the drinks, we order our food, and after another a little wait, I finally hear the sizzle of Kasie's steak fajitas coming out first. The amazing smell of the smoke coming off them has me wishing I ordered fajitas instead of enchiladas.

"And here are the enchiladas," the waitress says as she comes my way. "This plate is very hot, so be careful."

I thank her, and she continues passing out the rest of the food until everyone has their meal. We begin eating, and my dad starts telling one of his fishing stories, apparently prompted by his fish tacos.

I grab my margarita and take a sip before glancing at Kasie, preparing to offer her a part of my enchiladas for one of her fajitas, but I notice she's got this blank expression on her face, just staring at her food. Her hand is on her stomach, she's bent slightly forward, and I can tell she's trying to focus on slowing her breath.

I place my hand on her thigh and feel bad when it makes her jump. "I'm sorry. Are you feeling all right, though?" I ask quietly.

I watch her struggle for another breath before she answers, still staring a hole in her plate, "I'm just feeling a little anxious."

"Do you want to head back to the room? We can go right now."

"No, I don't want to make a scene. I want to try and tough it out."

"Okay."

I reach for her hand beneath the table and rub the back of it with my thumb, hoping I can bring her a little comfort as she battles what's going on inside her head.

When she closes her eyes, I split my attention between the rise and fall of her chest and Dad's story.

After a minute, I feel Kasie's grip tighten. She shifts in her seat before looking at me, her face full of worry. In between shallow breaths, she says, "Donnie, I'm having a hard time calming down. It's too loud in here, and I feel like I'm going to have a panic attack if I don't get some place where I can focus."

"Okay, let's get you back to the room."

Sadness clouds her features. "I'm sorry. I'm so embarrassed to have to leave like this."

"You won't be the reason we have to go," I say before reaching across the table to grab the salt. When I do, I intentionally knock my fishbowl margarita over and let it spill right into my lap, soaking my clothes. "Ah, shit!"

"Oh no!" my mom exclaims as everyone at our table turns towards Kasie and I.

"Damn, bro, are you drunk already?" Connor grins, and I glare at him jokingly.

The staff are quick to come over to help and offer me another drink.

"No, thank you," I say. "But I need to get out of these wet clothes. Can you guys box up our meal and have it delivered to our room?"

Our waitress nods, and I apologize for the mess before she makes her way to get the to-go boxes.

I interlock my fingers with Kasie's when she stands up, and the relief on her face is worth the ice-cold shock that I just gave myself.

After we excuse ourselves, we begin the walk to our room.

"I'm so sorry, Donnie. I just"—she pauses and takes a shallow breath—"my heart feels like it's coming out of my chest, and I'm shaky and tingly and—"

"Hey, you're okay, Kase. I'm not upset. You don't have to apologize. Do you have any idea what triggered you to feel this way, though?"

"I don't know!" She covers her face and throws her back against the hallway wall, sliding to a seated position. "I hate being like this, Donnie," she sniffles as I take a seat next to her and wrap my arm around her. She lays her head on my shoulder. "I feel so fucking stupid." She sniffles again, and the way her voice breaks when she's sad, it's like a knife in my chest.

"Why do you feel stupid?"

"Because I don't understand why I panic like this. I was just fine, and then I got in my head and couldn't get out. The walls started closing in, everyone got really loud, and I felt like if I passed out, no one would even know, and they wouldn't be able to help me if they *did* know. I would just lay there, helpless, gasping for breath. It's such an irrational scenario. It makes no fucking sense, right? Yet, to me, when I'm going through it, it makes perfect sense. It's so stupid. I'm scared of something that can't even hurt me."

I hold her tight. "You're not stupid, not even close. You have more resilience and mental toughness than you're giving yourself credit for. These panic attacks and this anxiety you feel, yeah, maybe they're still there, but they don't control you the way they used to, right? From what you've told me, they used to be in control, but the Kasie I've known for the last couple of years, she's the one in control. Yeah, you'll slip up every now and then, of course, but that's okay. Shit, you may look it, but you're not perfect. No one is."

She chuckles softly and lifts her head off my shoulder, staring at me with her pretty, wet eyes. "Did you really just call me perfect?"

I did.

And it's supposed to be kind of a light-hearted joke to make her laugh, but why do I mean it? Why am I watching her studying my eyes with hers, wishing she wasn't my fake girlfriend? Why do I want her to be mine?

She interrupts my thoughts, not waiting for me to answer her question when she says, "Thank you, Donnie. Thank you for not telling me to 'just get over it' or that I'm overreacting. I'm thankful that in my weakest moments, even though you have no idea what it's like to go through a panic attack, you build me up."

She kisses my shoulder with her soft lips, grabs hold of my arm tighter, snuggling closer as we sit in the hallway together, and it warms my entire body. I swear, this right here, *this* is perfect to me, wet lap and all.

Chapter Nine

Kasie

~ Day 5, Thursday ~

It's a new day, and the warm sun shining on my face through the bedroom windows is a refreshing way to wake up. I'm excited because today is shopping day. I want to find a new dress for Mila's bachelorette party—and maybe some other things, if anything catches my eye—and Donnie is looking for a new hat and sunglasses to wear to the bachelor party.

And he doesn't know it yet, but I'm also planning to do something special for him. The way he went above and beyond for me last night, it was completely unexpected. Spilling an ice-cold drink in his lap to keep everyone's eyes and attention away from me, that's crazy and so sweet. And being there for me the way he was and always is, it makes me feel special. So, I'm going to show him how much I appreciate him—fingers crossed that everything goes the way I expect it to.

Just another minute and I'll get out of bed.

There's something about this morning, lying in bed, it's extra cozy. Probably because I fell asleep in Donnie's arms last night, so I'm still snuggled close to him. I pull the blanket up to my neck and hug it against me as I scoot back against Donnie's warm body.

"Oh my gosh!" I exclaim, quickly flipping over when I feel something stiff and hard.

Donnie jolts awake and falls off the edge of the bed, because apparently, I somehow took up ninety percent of the bed last night. My reaction was probably more theatric than it needs to be, but it caught me by surprise and—well, whatever, I can't take it back.

"What the hell?" he groans, sprawled on the hardwood floor.

"I'm so sorry! Oh my gosh, I didn't mean to freak out. I just wasn't expecting to feel your—"

He looks at me, perplexed, and then widens his eyes when it hits him. "Oh shit, my bad," he says, standing up now and covering himself with his hands. "You fell asleep in my arms and I—"

"No, it's okay. I… Um, wow. I think I'm…going to go shower," I say with flushed cheeks and rasped breath, trying not to stare at him, but it's in my line of sight right now, and I've got morning brain, so… "Yeah, I'm going to go shower."

I make one more not-on-purpose glance at his hands doing their best to suppress how hard he is beneath his shorts this morning and hurry to the bathroom to shower—and to get ahold of myself.

When I close the bathroom door, I back up against it and squeeze my eyes shut.

"I cannot believe that just happened," I say beneath my breath.

Shopping has been a welcome breath of fresh air today. Donnie and I haven't had to pretend we're dating, so it's been nice to just hang out with my best friend in public again without looking over our shoulders and trying to make sure our performances are on point.

We stop in at a local dress shop, and I sift through racks of pretty dresses, picking an armful—and some matching accessories—to try on. I choose a fitting room and try on the first dress.

"What do you think about this one?" I ask Donnie as I step out and spin around so he can see the whole look.

"Hmm, I think for a bachelorette party, you've got to go sexier."

"Oh, do you?" I smirk.

"Yeah, what about that last one you chose?"

"That's a lingerie dress, Donnie."

"Ohhhh." He laughs and then stops. "Wait a minute…" He gets this curious look on his face.

"It's not for out here," I say, giggling. "And I'm not trying it on for you either. I don't need you getting hard again," I joke before turning back around and shutting the door to try the next dress on.

"You're mean! I was sleeping, Kasie," he defends.

I laugh and ignore his defense as I begin slipping out of the dress and into the next one. "Hey, so, we're not doing anything tomorrow morning, are we?"

"Not that I know of, why?"

I zip up the dress and put the big fancy hat I picked out with it on. I step out and pose like I'm at fashion shoot. "Is this sexy enough for you?" I ask, tugging at the ends of my hat and looking at him over my shoulder, being as theatrical as possible.

He laughs and shakes his head. "Why are you like this?"

I catwalk towards him with a sultry look in my eyes. "Whatever do you mean?" I ask, throwing a fancy flair into my voice. "This is just who I am, darling." I wrap one arm around his neck and jump into his arms, trusting he'll catch me and not let me fall to the floor, although, I can't say I'd blame him if he let me drop. On cue, he catches me and just stares at me, smiling into my soul.

"What? Why are you looking at me like that?"

"I don't know," he says, narrowing his eyes, and then he changes the subject. "So, why did you ask if we're free tomorrow?"

He sets me down and I smooth down my dress. "I wanted to do something special for you."

"Special for me? Why?"

"Because you turned yourself into a walking margarita last night to take the attention off me. And you're always there for me. So, I just wanted to do something to make you feel as special as you make me feel."

"Aww, Kasie." He wraps me into his arms and kisses the side of my head. "Now it's my turn to bombard you with kisses."

I laugh. "But you don't even know what it is yet."

"It doesn't matter. It's from you, and that's enough."

I smile and tuck my hair behind my ear. "So, I found this fishing trip that leaves tomorrow morning. It's a four-hour sail, and you could catch a whole bunch of different types of fish. They've got an open bar and a deck for relaxing. It sounds really cool, so I want to book it for you. And maybe you could ask your brother or your dad to go or something? Make it a little guys' trip since you all like fishing?"

He places his hands on my hips. "What about you?"

"Oh, I'll be fine. I can find something to do here while you guys are out."

"No, I meant, what if I asked *you* to go with me?"

"Me? But I don't know the first thing about fishing. Fun fact: the one and only time I've ever gone, I was with my dad, and the second I felt a fish bite my line, I tossed my fishing pole into the lake because it scared me."

He cracks up with laughter. "Why can I picture that so easily?" I look at him, unimpressed, and fold my arms across my chest. He reels in his laughter and says, "No, but for real, would you go? I think it would be fun to go together. Plus, now I'd kind of like to see a reenactment of you tossing your pole into the water." He chuckles and backs up, but not before I smack his arm.

"Do you really want me to go? You're not just saying it to be nice?"

"I really want you to go."

I sigh happily. "Okay. But now I need to find a fishing outfit too."

He groans, and now I bet he regrets asking me to go, but I just spin around happily and continue trying on the potential bachelorette party dresses.

I've got the perfect bachelorette party dress and accessories to go with it, the cutest fishing outfit for tomorrow—a fitted, striped T-shirt to go under a pair of white overall shorts, big sunglasses, and a pretty, white hat—and lot of other things I don't need but want in the shopping bags that are on the ground next to our table at this little outdoor café. Donnie's got his hat and sunglasses, as well as a matching fishing outfit that I bought for him and am fairly convinced he'll wear, so now we're having drinks to top the day off.

"So, who do you think is most likely to get you guys in trouble during the bachelor party?" I ask, swirling my straw around in my drink.

"Easy, that would be Nate. You know how there's always that one cousin who your parents wish you wouldn't spend so much time with, because they're always getting you into trouble and shit? That's Nate."

"Oh, no. Should I be worried?" I say, jokingly.

"Nah, he's harmless. He just has a knack for saying the wrong thing at the wrong time and then we have to get him out of whatever trouble his mouth got him into."

I chuckle softly and then say, "You know, if I'm being honest, the person I *am* worried about meeting is your ex."

"Why's that?"

"I don't know. I guess maybe because I

don't really know what to expect when I meet her. She's like the one topic you never talk about. And I feel like I need to be in best-friend-defense-mode around her, so I kind of wish I had an idea of who I'm up against."

Donnie takes a sip of his beer. "I don't want you to be in defense mode. I want you to enjoy your time out here. If you have your defenses up, you can't do that. Plus, you're not a mean girl."

"I can be mean," I say, frowning.

He smirks, and it makes the frown slip off my face.

Ugh, how does he do that?

"You're sweet, Kasie. Thank you for being ready to go to bat for me. But you probably won't even have to, because, like you, she's not mean either. And I really don't think she's here to stir anything up. I'll say this, if she hasn't changed, she's friendly but quiet, observant but not judgmental, and most definitely not confrontational."

"Oh… So, we don't hate her?" I ask, narrowing my eyes like I'm confused. Donnie facepalms and I laugh, grabbing his rugged hand

and pulling it toward me. "I'm kidding, Donnie. Thank you. That's at least enough information about her to calm my nerves. And even though I don't like her, I'm glad I don't have to be a total bitch. It's hard trying to be something you're not, you know?"

Our waiter drops off our rum shots.

"Yeah, I get it. I'm sorry that I dragged you into this fake dating shit. I can't help but wonder if that's what caused your anxiety to stir up last night."

"I don't know, maybe?" I shrug my shoulders. "But it's okay. Pretending to be your girlfriend is the easy part. Like, I-could-get-used-to-this kind of easy. I mean, I'm not saying I'm going to get used to it, but if you need me to do this again…" I pause to wink at him, and he scoffs.

"Seriously though, that's not the hard part. The hard part is putting on this show and seeing how much everyone adores it and then remembering that it's not going to have a happy ending. It feels mean. So maybe you're right; I hate confrontation, and being mean is confrontation's cousin."

Donnie sighs and fidgets in his chair while his expression turns downcast. "Yeah, I guess I didn't really think it through. I should have just been honest from the jump instead of being a selfish, lying asshole."

"No, I agreed to it too, so I'm just as much a part of this as you are. Whatever backlash is coming, we go through it together. I'm your ride or die," I say, laughing gently.

"Well, I do appreciate you doing this and being so cool about it. When this is all over, I owe you."

"Just wear the matching outfit I picked for you for tomorrow, and we'll call it even."

He groans. "Do I have to?"

"Yes," I whine.

Chapter Ten

Donnie

~ Day Six, Friday ~

We board the fishing boat and set sail with cocktails at 8 a.m.—nothing says vacation like drinking in the morning. We mingle among the rest of the passengers who are on the fishing excursion and eventually come to the spot where we'll be casting our lines. It takes quite a while before we get our poles set and actually cast out.

"Okay, now, if you get a bite, please don't throw your pole over the side of the boat," I plead with Kasie.

She shoves me and gives me a dirty look. "I'm not six anymore, smartass. *But* you are going to have to help me reel it in if I get one."

I nod, and before long, she gets the bite she was so worried about. I can't even tell if her squeal was happy or scared, or a mix of both.

"Ahh, it's so beautiful!" she exclaims when the mahi-mahi breaches the cobalt blue water and shows off its green and yellow color before splashing back beneath the surface.

I'm behind her, helping as much as I can until she wins the battle and brings the fish into the boat. The crew helps us weigh it—a twenty-five pounder—and they take a picture of her holding the fish, and it is about as long as she is.

She's got this beaming smile, and lately, it hits different. As I watch her interacting with the crew member who is helping her release the fish back into the ocean, my stomach knots, somersaults, fills with butterflies…I don't know what the fuck it's doing. But something is happening, and maybe I'm just afraid to admit that I know what it is, because it makes it more real.

No, I don't accept this. I don't accept that I'm falling for my best friend. It's infatuation or some shit. It will fade. It has to.

But it feels like I'm lying to myself, because over the last couple of days, I'm longing for moments like this, when she steals my breath away by just being her. My body aches for her. I'm craving her kisses, and I'm doing things just to see her smile. I swear, I'm losing it.

It's getting harder to ignore, but I keep reminding myself that the last time I wanted something more than what I had with someone special that I lost that person—Olivia. The last thing I want to do is put our friendship in jeopardy all because I fell for our act. So, again, I remind myself.

Bury the feelings as far down as you can. Enjoy this while we're out here, but you cannot feel, not for her. Accept it and leave well enough alone.

Chapter Eleven

Kasie

Two days later...

~ Day 8, Sunday ~

I'm lying in bed on my side, with the covers up over my shoulder. I can hear Donnie's even breathing while I stare at the text that I've been contemplating sending to Morgan for the last five minutes.

[Me]: Girl, I messed up. I need you to talk some sense into me.

I'm not even sure I want to tell her, but if I don't tell her, I'm going to tell Donnie, and that's something I'm not sure I'm ready for. And I'm certain *he's* not ready for it.

Fuck it, just send it.

I click the send button and take a deep breath, trying to figure out how best to explain what's going on in my head and in my heart when I'm not even really sure myself.

[Morgan]: Call me?

No, I need time to process my thoughts before spouting off the wrong thing.

[Me]: It's okay, I can text you.

[Morgan]: All right, what's up, girl?

I can't believe I'm doing this. Am I really doing this?

I have half a mind to back out but decide not to.

[Me]: I think I might have feelings for Donnie. Like, romantic feelings.

Wow, this is really happening.

If I didn't believe what I was feeling was real before, it definitely feels that way now, with the words staring me in the face.

I watch the three bubbles that tell me she's responding appear on the screen and then disappear, appear again, and then disappear once more. I can only imagine what she is typing, erasing, and retyping.

Ugh, why is this happening to me? This was the one thing that I was never supposed to experience with him.

When the bubbles disappear a third time, my phone vibrates and scares the shit out of me.

She's calling.

I hurry carefully out of the covers and slowly open the sliding glass door to the patio before stepping out to answer her call, "Hey, girl," I say nonchalantly as goosebumps begin to cover my arms and legs. The evening breeze is stronger and cooler tonight, making me wish I was wearing something other than a tank top and these short pajama shorts.

"Uh-uh, don't 'hey girl' me like you didn't just drop that truth bomb on me. You're fucking with me, right?"

"I wish I was. Umm, hold on though." I can't take it, I'm too chilly to concentrate on this conversation. I pop my head back in and sneak Donnie's denim jacket off the back of the chair near the patio door and slip it on. I'm surrounded by distressed denim and his sandalwood scent, which makes me wish I was back in bed, snuggled in the warmth of his strong arms. When I close the door back, I fill Morgan in on our fake relationship: the kissing, the flirty moments, the sweet moments…the kissing.

"I can't be falling for him, Morgan."

"You're right—"

"Good. So, you think I'm reading too much into it too—"

"No, what I meant is, you're right, you can't be falling for him because you already fell."

"No," I whine, tilting my head back and staring hopelessly at the bottom of the balcony above our patio.

"Oh, yes. You're in deep, Kasie. But it's not necessarily a bad thing."

"What do you mean it's not a bad thing? He trusted me to play this fake girlfriend role without catching feelings, and now I've gone and done that." I sit on the patio chair and double over, burying my face in my palms.

"Did he actually tell you not to catch

feelings?"

"No. Not specifically."

"Well then you're good."

"No, I'm horrible. I was so afraid his ex being out here would screw with his head, but if I tell him that I'm falling for him, it's me who's going to do that."

"Okay, to be honest, he's had enough grieving time over his first love. It's time to fucking move on. I mean, shit, it's not like she died."

"Morgan!" I gasp, sitting back up and looking over my shoulder to make sure my surprised voice didn't just wake Donnie up.

"What? It's true. If he doesn't want to date, that's just fine. But how long is he going to use *her* as an excuse for why he can't? Anyways, aside from worrying that he's going to freak, I want to know how *you* feel about these feelings? Besides 'extra horny?'" She chuckles, and I knew I shouldn't have told her I said that.

"Listen, in my defense, at the time, I thought I was just horny. But I've since realized that being extra horny was just a side effect from beginning to fall for him."

"Yeah, I mean, I can't believe you pleasured yourself to him. The fact that you guys haven't had spontaneous sex is beyond me."

"Umm, first off, I did not *pleasure myself* to him. He just kind of showed up in my thoughts—uninvited, I might add. Anyway," I say with a sigh, jokingly annoyed, "these feelings, they have me excited *and* scared. I've tried denying what I'm feeling but I can't help it; I want him. But I also don't want to complicate things, you know? What we have is so good—"

"Of course, I understand. But you guys are close, and Donnie is so chill. I'd be willing to bet that if he isn't feeling the same way you are—although it sounds to me like he is, or he wouldn't have admitted that he likes kissing you—then you guys could be adults and work it out."

"Yeah, maybe you're right."

A collage of memories from this trip replay in my head. The one thing that holds true through each one is that there's not a person in this world that I would rather share them with than him. The way he cares for me, the way he keeps me laughing and smiling, the way he makes me feel alive, it's unmatched—and honestly, I don't know what shifted, because it's always been this way, but I want to be his girl.

"I'm definitely right. Now, my closing argument for you to tell him how you feel is this: imagine some other girl coming into his life and telling him how she feels, and then they get fucking married. And you're on the sidelines, wondering if you ever had a shot, all because you didn't speak up. It's not like you to stay silent, Kasie. So, say something. Either way, no matter what happens, at least you'll know."

I sigh deeply. "Okay, I'll sleep on it. Tomorrow evening, we've got a sushi date planned, so if the conversation is going to happen, it'll be during dinner."

"Perfect. That'll be nice, quiet, and intimate. I like it. And you better fill me in!"

I giggle softly. "I will. Thanks, girl."

"Anytime."

We say our goodbyes and I sneak back inside the room and slide into bed, sitting against the headboard, staring like a creeper at Donnie's handsome face as he sleeps. If he were to open his eyes right now, this would be so awkward. But his expression is peaceful, so I get to sit back and admire the guy I've called my best friend for the last two years and wonder if I could ever call him my for-real boyfriend.

Please don't hate me for having these feelings, Donnie. I didn't mean for this to happen, I swear. Falling for you is the hardest, most effortless thing I've ever done.

Chapter Twelve

Donnie

~ Day 9, Monday ~

After lunch with the family, Connor, Mila, Kasie, and I head over to the tiki bar for a couple drinks before the girls go shopping for the day.

Kasie is at the bar paying her tab when I feel someone clap my arm and a familiar voice belt out, "What's up, douchebags?"

I turn around and my favorite cousin, Nate, is standing there in his pink polo shirt with his hair slicked and a Cheshire cat smile.

"Oh, hell no. I thought you weren't coming in until the bachelor party on Wednesday?"

"Crypto investing, man. I'm telling you, that's where it's at. I made ten Gs on one trade. I figured I'd spend it on a couple extra days with my favorite cousins before the wedding pops off."

"Ten Gs? How much have you lost, though?" Connor jests.

"Hey, are you guys happy to see me or not?"

"Well, I am," Mila pipes up and wraps him in a hug.

"At least someone is," Nate chuckles, and then checks out the scene, sighing happily. "Man, I am in love with this place. I've never seen so many fine-ass girls in one spot." He stops his gaze at the bar. "Like right there, at twelve o'clock." He points at Kasie, who just finished paying and is now walking toward us.

The wind plays with her hair, and she smiles at the ground when she notices us looking her way.

"Yeah, she's one in a million," I say, mesmerized by her, not even realizing that he doesn't know she's my girl yet because he doesn't have any social media accounts.

"I can tell that pussy is fire. You know she got that cream," Nate says, nudging me with his elbow. "Like you'd be deep inside of her, and she'd have your toes curling and shit."

"Well, too bad for you," Connor says. "That's Donnie's girl."

Nate scoffs. "Fuck that. Donnie doesn't even date. You can't call dibs for him."

I start to clarify, "No, he means—"

"Shut up, she's almost here." He adjusts his shirt and seconds later Kasie reaches us. "What's up, girl?"

Kasie looks confused, and I step in to clear up the confusion. "Nate, this is my *girlfriend*, Kasie. Kasie, this is my cousin, Nate."

Nates face turns beet red, and Connor, Mila, and I crack up laughing.

"What did I miss?" Kasie asks with a quirk of her brow as she and Nate shake hands.

"You don't want to know," I say with a snort.

She giggles. "Okay, well, it's nice to meet you, Nate. Mila, are you ready to go?"

"Yep. You boys stay out of trouble." She points a stern finger at all of us. "Especially you, Nate." She grins.

"What, why do I get singled out? I'm not trouble."

"Mmhmm."

Kasie hugs me and stands on her tiptoes to give me a quick kiss that I wish was longer.

I swear her lips get softer every day.

It's another thought I shouldn't have. But I'm getting used to them, and every time I feel myself crumble for her, I have to build myself back up. Although, every time I do, I feel like I'm built back weaker, because it's taking less and less to knock me down.

"Oh, and baby," she says, looking back over her shoulder. "Don't forget about our sushi date at six o'clock tonight. I have something special I want to tell you."

Something special? Hmm, I wonder what it could be.

I nod and smile, and the girls are off.

Nate claps my shoulder and snaps me out of the trance I didn't know I was in while watching her walk away. "Yeah, baby, don't forget about that

sushi date," he says, trying to sound sensuous—
which is weird—while winking.

I shake my head, ignoring his statement.
"Cream, bro? Really?"

"What? How was I supposed to know she
was your girl?" He shrugs.

"Well, if you had social media…"

"Eh, no thanks. But she got it like that
though, right?" He smirks, and I give him a shove
before we head to the bar to order drinks.

After a few hours go by, we're sitting
around the fire pit just outside the tiki bar, staring
out at the ocean, talking about old times. We're all a
little more buzzed than we should be when I hear
my text alert go off. I reach inside my pocket.

"Come on, D," Nate slurs. "You get to see
her every day. Do you really have to text her the

whole time she's gone, too? I'm only here for five days and then back to Michigan, and you're back to Cali."

"Alright, alright, shit." I switch my phone to silent mode from inside my pocket.

"Cut him some slack," Connor tells Nate. "They're still in that can't-keep-their-hands-off-of-each-other honeymoon stage."

I chuckle. "Bro, I don't want to hear it. You and Mila can't even hang out with us for a couple hours before you're sneaking back to your room."

"Hey, being out here is like a natural aphrodisiac. How do you think Mila convinced me to do a destination wedding?"

"Oh, yeah, I'm sure she had to do a lot of convincing," I say, laughing because I know he's wrapped around Mila's finger. Although, I can't say much, because Kasie's got me around hers, somehow, and we're not even really dating.

Another drunk hour goes by and the sunset that gave us a pretty blue and purple sky earlier is gone, leaving behind a dark, twinkling sky.

Nate looks at me with his eyes half open. "You're a lucky man, D. You really are."

"Oh yeah? Why's that?"

"Come on, that girl you're with, Masie—"

"Kasie," I correct him.

"That's what I said. Anyways, you're lucky because you've been out of the game for years and then you jump back in with this fucking baddie. You better not fuck it up, though, because I bet she's the type who will leave your ass in the dirt if you do."

"Man, shut up." I punch his arm. "And I'm not going to fuck it up." I chuckle and then it hits me. I *did* fuck up. "Shit! Kasie!" My eyes widen and my stomach sinks, panic filling every vein of my body as I shove my hand in my pocket, spilling my beer as I try to rush my phone out to check the time. A handful of missed calls and a bunch of texts wondering where I am are staring me in the face as

I stare at the number eight on the clock, wishing I can somehow change it back to a six but it's useless.

Shit, I'm dead. I stood her the fuck up, what the hell is wrong with me? How did I forget?

I jump up out of my seat and rush towards the sushi restaurant without saying a word to Connor or Nate. I reach the restaurant and frantically scan the dining area before asking the maître d if a pretty, blonde girl was in here a couple hours ago sitting alone, waiting on someone who never showed.

My heart splits in half when he nods and informs me that she didn't leave when I didn't show up. Instead, she sat at the table and ate by herself.

Ahh, I'm such an asshole. How the hell did I not feel my phone vibrating?

I thank him and hurry toward our room, hoping she is there but I have no idea what I'm going to say for myself if she is.

When I reach the room door, the key card slips out of my trembling hand to the floor.

All right, calm down. It's possible she's not

even as upset as you think she will be.

I pick up the room key off the ground, swipe it, and push the door open. As I step in, I shove my hand through my hair and take a deep breath, trying to prepare myself for whatever awaits.

I walk to the bedroom doorway and there she is, sitting on the bed, wearing a sports bra and sweatpants. The beautiful floral dress that she was excited to wear for our date is balled up on the floor next to her black heels, and it kills me a little more. The long, wavy hair that fell over her shoulders earlier in the day is now tied up into a messy ponytail. She looks cute, but sad, and she won't take her eyes off the TV.

"Hey…," I say, carefully like a child who knows he did something wrong and is trying to sound as innocent as possible to avoid a harsher punishment.

It feels like an hour passes before she responds. "Did you forget something?" she asks, examining her fingernails rather than looking at my guilty face. I wish she would look at me so she can see how sorry I am and how horrible I feel.

I swallow uncomfortably. "Kasie, I'm so

sorry. I didn't—"

"They had this roll that came out on fire. It was really cool. You would have loved it."

I'm sure I would have. Except, I know she's not telling me about it to get me hyped, because her tone isn't bubbly, and her face isn't lit up.

"Are you mad at me?" I squeeze my eyes shut and internally smack my forehead.

What a dumb question to ask right now. What do you think, dumbass?

"No. I'm not mad, Donnie. I'm just disappointed."

Why does that somehow make me feel worse?

She continues, "Did you have fun?"

That's a question that sends alarm bells straight to my brain. You don't answer that honestly. Not at a time like this. "No."

"No? So, you stood me up, and you weren't even having fun?"

Should I just walk my face into the wall?

"Well… I mean, I… It—"

She creases her brows, snaps her eyes to mine, and I wish I could say those beautiful, brown eyes steal my breath for a good reason, but not this time. "Don't answer how you think I want you to answer, Donnie. Just tell me honestly. I don't want you to lie to me because you think it will make me feel better."

She gives my breath back as she takes her eyes off me and focuses them back on the TV.

"I'm sorry, you're right. I've never lied to you before, so why start now? Yes, I did enjoy catching up with my cousin."

"Ok. Well, I'm glad you had fun." She gets up off the bed, grabbing her blanket and pillow. "I'm going to get some sleep."

"Wait, let me sleep on the couch. I deserve it."

"No. It's fine, Donnie. Just take the bed. I'll see you in the morning."

"Kase," I say, moving out of the way as she passes me without a word or a glance. "Kasie."

Still no response.

I hang my head and strip down to my boxers, sighing as I get into bed. As the minutes pass, the fresh, rose petal scent from Kasie's side of the bed is slowly fading. I turn to my stomach and hug my pillow, trying not to focus on how cold and empty the room feels without her.

There is no way I'm going to sleep well tonight.

~ Day 10, Tuesday ~

My tired eyes creep open to the sound of Kasie's blow dryer running. After a minute or so, I grab my phone and check the time—7 a.m. I chuckle to myself, betting that she's purposely being loud enough to wake me up—well deserved, obviously—because she normally waits until at least eight. I pick my head up off my pillow and sneak a look into the bathroom, trying to get a glimpse of her face, like it'll somehow tell me how upset she still is. My eyes widen when I see her standing there, angled slightly towards me in these sexy, pink lace panties and a matching bra. And *she's got heels on.*

Woah. Damn, Kasie.

My eyes trail her body, and it's way too early to fight my cock stiffening inside my boxers. I try looking away, but it's no use. I can't peel my eyes off her. The wrong head takes over, and I start to imagine what's underneath her bra and panties. I've never seen her naked, but something about her glow this morning makes me curious. She glances over at me like she can feel me staring, and I turn away, feeling like a perv.

She doesn't react to catching me staring.

When she's done drying her hair, she walks leisurely over to the closet and starts sifting through outfits. When her back is turned, I hurry off the bed and slide on a pair of jeans so I can hide how hard she's got me. As I'm zipping my pants, she comes out from the closet, holding a yellow dress in her hands.

"I don't feel like faking it today, so I'm going to do my own thing. If anyone asks about me, just make up an excuse for why I'm not around," she says, walking to the bathroom and shutting the door behind her.

"O...kay," I drawl, even though she didn't wait for my response.

A few minutes go by before she comes out of the bathroom, wearing the short, strapless dress she chose. A twinge of envy for any guy who lays eyes on her today stings me.

"You look gorgeous."

"Thank you." She grabs her phone, room key, and purse. "See ya," she says, walking out of the room without giving me so much as another glance.

When I hear the door close, I take a seat on the bed and fall backward into a sea of king-sized blankets and sheets. "Ahh, this sucks. I'm such an idiot," I groan aloud, staring at the white ceiling.

After a bit, I sit back up and grab my phone to send her a text.

[Me]: Kasie, I'm really sorry that I didn't show up last night. I know I let you down, but I hope you can forgive me and let me make it up to you.

I toss my phone on my pillow, assuming she won't text back right now because I know she works through things by distancing herself and being alone. I never thought I'd be on the receiving end, because I'm usually her safe haven when she needs to get away from pushy boyfriends or flaky friends. I'm usually the one who brings her smile back and makes her laugh uncontrollably. The one who holds and comforts her when she needs it. Whatever it is, I'm always there. And now, being the one who hurt her, I've never felt worse. The guilt is just gnawing away at my stomach.

I grab my blanket off the bed, wrap it around myself, make a cup of coffee, and sit on the patio, staring at the ocean. I start trying to figure out ways that I can make Kasie feel special again, but I end up spaced out for so long that my neglected coffee gets cold. As much as I'd love to sit here and let the day inch by, I have to get ready to have breakfast at the café with Connor, Mila, and Nate. So, I grab some beers from the mini fridge and have a couple of shower beers while staring right through the water hitting my body.

When I get to the café, I find their table and walk up, glancing at the empty chair that would be Kasie's, and the knot in my stomach tightens.

"Where's Kasie?" Mila asks.

"Yeah, your ass just took off last night after you yelled her name." Nate chuckles before taking a gulp of water.

"I'm in the doghouse, guys" I say as I take my seat and explain what happened.

"Fuck, my bad, bro," Nate says when I finish. "This wouldn't have happened if I didn't give you shit for being on your phone."

"No, it's not your fault, man. This is on me."

"So, what are you going to do about it?" Connor asks.

"I don't know yet. It's eating me up inside, though."

"Well, good, it should be." Mila crosses her

arms and shoots me with a scowl.

"Damn, come on, Mila, I didn't mean to do it."

"I know, but it doesn't take away from the fact that you hurt her. I'm sorry, but you've got this amazing girl who adores you. And I swear, you guys literally have the sweetest relationship. So, please, please, please, don't fuck it up by being a typical douchebag guy, D, because I swear if you turn her into your rebound girl, I will kick your ass. She's wifey material."

"She's not my rebound—"

"Then pull yourself together and figure out what you're going to do to make it right. Just don't be annoying. Let her have her space today, and then when she's ready, listen to her and be there for her."

"All right. I will."

Chapter Thirteen

Kasie

I've been strong all day, but I'm three island sangrias deep and my strength is fading. It doesn't help that every song in this stupid lounge sounds like heartbreak. All I want to do is cry and be in my feelings, because it feels like I just got dumped by my first love over text, which is stupid because it's not that on any level, but the hurt is there. And what's worse is the person who I usually lean on when I'm sad is the one who made me that way. I know he didn't mean to. And not showing up to our sushi dinner last night wouldn't be a big deal under normal circumstances— annoying, yes, but normally I would just give him shit and make him make it up to me and move on, but this wasn't just another dinner date. I hyped myself up to bare my soul last night, specifically told him I had something special to tell him so that he would know how important the date was, and all that confidence and hope I felt went up in flames right along with my sushi.

Why didn't he just show up? It has to be a sign that telling him would have been catastrophic to our friendship. I mean, we stole a kiss that wasn't meant for appearances the other day, and the ocean waves pushed us apart. And then, I decide I'm going to tell him that I want to date for real and he stands me up, which has never happened before.

"You can't tell me that's not a sign," I mutter to myself, before resting my elbow on the bar and my chin in my palm, swirling the straw in my drink around.

I just need a day away from him to sulk and drink my sorrows away. After this, I'll be fine. I have to be.

My text alert dings.

Please don't be from Donnie.

But of course, it's from him and seeing his stupid smiling contact photo makes my heart ache all over again.

This really hurts.

I sniffle, and a tear escapes from the corner of my eye and slides down my cheek. I should wipe it before someone notices I'm sitting here alone and crying, but I'm frozen.

I contemplate putting my phone away without reading what he wrote, but screw it.

[Donnie]: Hey Kase, I know you're still mad at me, and you definitely don't have to respond to me right now because I know you want your space. I just didn't know what your plans were for the day, so I put this playlist together for you. I filled it with a bunch of songs that mean something to us. I figured it would be nice to have some happy memories today. I love you, Kasie. And I miss you.

Seconds later, a playlist titled "Our Memories" comes through.

My stomach flips, and another tear falls while I scroll through the list of songs, replaying the cherished memories that put them there: the screaming duets on our long road trips, the best friend anthems that we dedicated to each other, and the hype songs he always plays while we get ready to go out. So many smiles, so much hearty laughter, so many reasons to run back to our room, jump in his arms, forgive him, bury my selfish feelings, and be thankful for the version of him that I *do* have.

"Nice ink," murmurs a deep voice from

behind me, interrupting my thoughts. A pair of tattooed arms rest on the bar next to me.

I hurry and wipe the tears away and turn my head to see a handsome stranger with honey eyes smiling at me and nodding at the butterfly tattoo on my shoulder blade.

"Oh, thank you." I smile softly. "Yours are nice too," I say before turning back to my drink.

"Thanks." He orders a beer from the bartender and then says, "Is there a story behind it?"

As much as I'd like to end this conversation right now and continue sulking alone, I suppose it's helping me keep my mind off Donnie and my crushed heart, so what the hell?

I nod and toy with the ends of my hair. "When I was eighteen, I had a traumatic experience that forced me to abruptly move away from my hometown. I got this tattoo to symbolize the promise I made to myself that I would take control and become a stronger version of me."

"That's deep. I like that." He takes a gulp of his beer and then extends his hand. "I'm Damen."

"Kasie," I say, placing my hand in his firm

grip.

"It's nice to meet you, Kasie. I hope you don't mind me standing here, by the way. I'm just waiting on some friends."

"No, you're okay. I *will* warn you though. I'm nursing a broken heart, so I probably won't be the most exciting company."

"Ah, that's no good. A broken heart out here in paradise?"

I force a small smile and ask. "So, what are you out here for?"

"Just a little getaway with friends. Nothing big. You?"

"My best friend's brother's wedding."

"All right, that's what's up. You need a plus one? I swear I'm not a creeper." He grins, and it makes me giggle. He takes a small step backward and plants his hand on his chest, pretending to be offended. "What, you don't believe me?"

"No, I believe you. I'm pretty good at spotting creepers these days. My DMs are full of them."

"Really?"

I nod and take a sip of my cocktail. "Oh yeah, I've got it all. Dick pics, marriage proposals from guys I've never met, guys cussing me out for not responding to their very forward sexual advances. It's a madhouse. Sometimes, my best friend and I get drunk and just read through the messages and laugh our asses off."

My smile fades and my heart squeezes at the thought, because in my mind's eye, I can see Donnie smiling at me, and I can hear his laughter. I'm seriously missing him so much.

"Uh-oh," Damen says. "Is your best friend the source of that broken heart?"

"It's kind of my own fault. I knew the rules."

"Rules?"

I sigh gently. "For personal reasons, my best friend doesn't do relationships, and his family doesn't get it, but I do. Which is why I agreed to join him on this trip as his fake girlfriend, to keep them off his back. The only problem is, at some point, things got real for me."

"And they didn't for him?"

"Well, technically…I don't know. I never got the chance to tell him how I was feeling."

He furrows his brows as a confused expression dawns on his face. "Okay, I'm not trying to be all up in your business, but if you never told him, then what's the deal with the broken heart?"

How did I get into this conversation with a stranger?

"I'm sorry. I should stop talking. I'm sure you did *not* come in here to listen to some sad girl blab on about her problems. Not to mention, I don't even know you."

"Hey, sometimes it's easier to unpack your feelings with a stranger. No biased judgments and shit, you know?" I start with another excuse to be quiet, but he interrupts, "Plus, my life is boring as hell, and yours clearly isn't." He smirks and I roll my eyes, cracking a contemptuous smile.

"So, this is entertaining for you?"

He turns to the bartender and says, "Two shots, please." And then he turns back to me. "Don't change the subject. I'm invested now. Lay it on me."

I twist my chair towards him and place my hands in my lap. "Fine. The reason he doesn't know how I feel is because I worked up the courage to tell him over a dinner that he never showed up to. He got drunk with his brother and cousin and lost track of time, so, our chance to be together was lost too."

"But you don't know if he's feeling you. And he doesn't know you're feeling him. So, maybe there's still a chance."

Our shots arrive, and we clink the shot glasses together before shooting them back.

I tuck locks of hair behind my ear. "No, I'm not going down that road again. I was hopeful yesterday, but today I'm realistic. I'm not happy about it, *but* my best friend does not want to date. I know that and I don't want to put that pressure on him. It's not fair. Not when I know what I know."

Damen scoffs. "I'm sorry, but you don't seem like the kind of girl who settles. I'd be willing to bet you make a lasting impression everywhere you go."

"Well, I hope I did this morning," I say beneath my breath, but apparently loud enough for him to hear, because he gives me a look that practically begs me to elaborate. "All right, this will test that no judgment thing, but I pranced around our room wearing sexy underwear, hoping to show him what he missed out on."

"How do you show him what he missed out on if he doesn't even know he has a shot?"

"Had a shot," I correct him. "And what's important is I got the reaction I wanted, okay?"

"Oh, I'm sure you did. You're fine as hell."

I laugh. "Thank you."

He turns his head, and so do I when we hear someone holler, "Yo, Damen!"

Damen waves at his friend and lifts his index finger to tell him he'll join their table in a second. "Come hang out with us," he tells me.

"It's okay. You go enjoy your vacation. I'll be fine. Thanks for talking with me, though."

"Of course. You're sure you don't want to hang though?" He asks with an inviting smile that makes me stop and think. "It beats sitting here drinking alone. You'd fit in with everyone and you're not the only girl."

"You know what? Sure, why not?"

It's almost two in the morning when I come stumbling down the quiet hallway, pretty intoxicated.

"You didn't have to walk me to my room. I would have been okay," I tell Damen.

"We're staying at the same resort. It's the least I could do. Plus, have you ever seen *Disappeared* on Investigation Discovery?"

"Oh my gosh," I slur. "I love that show, but it frustrates me to no end because every episode leaves me with more questions than answers. Like, I *need* a resolution," I groan.

"The girl needs her happy ending," he says and then nods at my room door.

The insistent smile on his face tells me he

isn't talking about the show anymore. Sadness rolls in as I move my gaze to the room key in my hand.

"Hey," Damen says, and I look up at him. "Don't give up hope. Tell him how you feel."

I force a smile. "We'll see. How about that?"

"That'll do." He chuckles.

"Thanks for walking me back. Have a good night, Damen." I step inside the dark room, give a small wave to him, and shut the door quietly behind me.

I look toward the couch and because of the glow from the TV, I can see Donnie cuddled up under the blanket. I sigh to myself, because I hate this spot that we're in. I about fall over trying to take off my heels, and when I finally get them off, I tiptoe to the bedroom, ready to lay down and pass out.

I switch on the light, and my heart melts in my chest as I try not to cry for the hundredth time today. Except, these tears are happier than the others, because for the first time today, I feel like Donnie and I will be just fine. In the middle of our made-up bed are a bouquet of colorful flowers, a handwritten letter, the coconut bikini top that I've wanted since the first day we got here and haven't been able to find, the cutest, softest-looking, little brown teddy bear with big puppy dog eyes that are begging to be forgiven, and tickets for us to go parasailing on Friday.

Butterflies zoom in my stomach as I pick up the handwritten letter and forego changing my clothes for now. I haven't received a handwritten letter since middle school, and having one now brings back that giddy feeling. I sit at the edge of the bed, wipe my wet eyes, and grab the teddy bear to accompany me as I read.

Kasie,

There are no words to describe the emptiness I felt spending today without you. I missed you so much. Your laugh, your bubbly smile, your energy—all of you. I guess I've always known this, but today really proved that you are the reason the sun shines in my life. And you are the reason I smile each day. I know it may be hard to believe after I didn't show up last night, but you are the most important person in my life. I'm sorry that I stole your smile away. I never meant to hurt you. When I asked you to be my girlfriend for two weeks,

I had every intention of being a good boyfriend to you. But last night, I was a terrible boyfriend, and even worse, I was a shitty best friend. I left you hanging, and that was not cool. I hope you can find it in your heart to forgive me. I won't ever take you for granted again, Kasie. I love you.

P.S. I went into town this afternoon and bought everything we need to make sushi together on Friday after parasailing. I've been watching YouTube videos all day, and I'm pretty confident that we can do the Fire Dragon Roll together without burning the whole resort down.

I set the letter down and fall to a fetal position on the bed, squeezing my teddy bear against my chest and crying as quietly as I can. It was only a matter of time before the dam behind my eyes broke. I feel like an emotional mess right now, but I need to let it all out because I can't hold onto this hurt anymore.

I'm sorry I fell for you, Donnie. This wasn't supposed to happen.

After the little waterfalls behind my eyes stop flowing, I pull myself together and change into a baggy T-shirt and boy shorts. I wipe my makeup off and look at myself in the bathroom mirror. My cheeks and nose are rosy, and my eyes are a little puffy. My throat still aches, but not as much as my heart.

I take a deep breath and give myself a hard look. "You can do this, Kasie," I say aloud. "Just because you lost your chance with him doesn't mean you lost him. He's still your person. And you're still his."

I get in bed and turn to my side, cuddling the teddy bear Donnie bought me while staring at his side of the bed.

All I want is for everything to go back to normal. I'll bury these feelings that I failed to drink away. I just need my best friend back. Eventually, I know I will be okay. It's just five more days. That's all I have to get through until our act is over. I guess, until then, I'll soak up every moment of being what I'll never truly be—his girlfriend.

The minutes pass like hours, and my tired eyes and racing mind won't cooperate enough to send me to sleep.

I can't do this anymore.

I get up out of bed and walk to the living room to wake Donnie.

Chapter Fourteen

Donnie

A gentle touch and quiet voice whispering my name wakes me up, and I see Kasie kneeling next to me.

"Hey," I exclaim gruffly, hoping I don't sound creepily excited but man, I missed her so much. All day long I've had this emptiness in the pit of my stomach, just waiting and aimlessly walking around the room, cleaning shit that didn't need to be cleaned in the first place. I'm pretty sure room service would be impressed with my level of detail. But being without her all day, it's put something into perspective for me: I'm lost without her.

"Hey… Can me and Mr. Snuggles join you? I don't want to be alone tonight."

"You already named him?"

"Of course I did," she giggles softly, and my

world continues piecing back together.

"Come here." I scoot against the back couch cushions, making room for her, and she surrenders into my arms, snuggling her back against my shirtless chest.

"I'm sorry if I smell like a mini-bar."

I laugh gently. "You're good, Kasie. Trust me. I'm just happy to hold you in my arms."

I kiss the back of her head, breathe her in, and wrap my arms around her, holding her as if I'll never let her go again. She kisses my arm softly, and within minutes, she's out.

This is dangerous; having the warmth of her soft, delicate body pressed against me right now, it makes me want to tell her things that I've been adamant about keeping to myself. I want to tell her that every time we touch, my heart beats faster, that every kiss leaves me craving more. That every time she gazes up into my eyes, I don't want this to be an act anymore. I'm crazy about her, and it scares me that I want her to know it. But what scares me even more is that I don't know what happens if she *does* know. What if I ruin our friendship, all because I wanted more? Or what if we do give it a shot but things don't work out, then what? I lost my best friend for a day, and it was tortuous. I don't even want to imagine losing her for a lifetime.

Sleep on it and we'll figure this shit out tomorrow.

~ Day 11, Wednesday ~

Sunshine invades our room, and the warmth of it against my skin wakes me up. The first thing I see is Kasie, fully dressed, walking back and forth from the bedroom to the living room, packing her beach bag. Her hair is wavy, and her makeup is flawless. And although I wish I woke to her wearing a lacy bra and panties again, she's got this cute, cozy look going on with her joggers, white cropped T-shirt, and her sweater jacket hanging off her shoulder.

For just a second, I imagine what it would be like if I went over there and gave her a surprise hug from behind. I'd squeeze her gently but firmly in my arms while I kiss her bare shoulder and up the back of her neck to her ear. She'd smile, put her hands on my forearms, and lean her head back against me. And in that moment, she'd be mine, and I'd be hers. We'd be more than just best friends.

It's too early for this.

I shake the thought away and come back to reality.

"Good morning," I say, sitting up and shoving my hand through my messy brown hair.

She looks over, and a smile splits her face. "Hey, good morning, sleepy head."

Oh, how I've longed to hear her say something familiar like that.

"What are you up to?"

"Just packing some things Mila said I'd need for the bachelorette party today. I hope you don't mind me letting you sleep in. I felt bad that I came in so late last night and woke you up and stuff."

"Well, considering you *never* let me sleep in when you're around, I'll relish in this moment."

I grin and she scrunches up her nose, glaring at me. I bet she doesn't even realize how fucking irresistible she looks when she does it.

I really am falling for you, aren't I?

"Yeah, well, don't get used to it," she jests, and it makes me chuckle. She grabs her beach bag off the dining table and walks towards me. "Okay, I have to get going."

I stand up to wrap her in a tight hug and she lays her head against my chest.

I wonder if she can feel my heart pounding.

After a moment, with her head still against me, she says, "Thank you for the sweet apology and for holding me last night. I'm sorry if it was weird, I just…I missed you, and I didn't—"

"I missed you too," I say before she tries explaining herself out of this moment. "It wasn't weird at all. It was…what we needed."

Well, that just made it weird. Why did I word it that way?

She looks up at me, and whatever's in her eyes, she doesn't say. "Yeah…so I'm going to go," she says, gesturing her thumb over her shoulder towards the door. "I'll probably see you some time tonight."

Yep, I definitely made it weird. Now she's rushing out.

Before I have any more time to think, she gives me a quick kiss on the cheek and starts for the door, leaving only the sexy scent of her perfume between us.

"Hey," I say, and she spins back around. "Are we good?"

"Yeah, of course," she says, smiling softly.

Then why does it feel like something is off?

Damn, it's like lately I can't even read my best friend. I've always been able to, but I don't know what's happening to me.

My buzzing phone cuts into the silence between us, and Kasie must use it as her cue because she heads for the door, glancing over her shoulder with a lopsided grin as she waves at me before disappearing into the hallway.

Okay, that was kind of flirty, right?

"I think I'm losing it," I say under my breath. "Fuck. What are you doing to me, Kasie?"

But my ringing phone doesn't give me time to think about that right now. So, I walk across the living room to grab it off the end table. It's Lavelle, one of the groomsmen.

I pick up the call. "What's up, Velle?"

"We just landed, bruh. You ready to kick this shit off?"

"Hell, yeah. Let me know when you guys get here. We'll have brunch and then hit our first stop right after."

"Listen to this guy. We'll have brunch,'" he mocks with a fancy accent, and I hear Marcus — another groomsman—in the background laughing along with him.

"Fuck you guys."

Even though I'm feeling a little off because of what happened with Kasie, I'd be lying if I said I wasn't excited to get this bachelor party started. Aside from Coach's funeral last year, we haven't had the group together like this in a while. After high school, Lavelle went off to a D1 college on a baseball scholarship and then went pro. Marcus and Gavin moved an hour away to go to college together, and Nate moved to Detroit for work. And after graduating from college and finishing my apprenticeship at a remodeling company, I moved to California on a glowing recommendation from my mentor and have been working my way up within a luxury home remodeling company ever since. Connor was the only one of us who stuck to his roots, where it all began.

I remember walking home under many sunsets trailing behind the group—they're all Connor's age—covered in dirt and dragging a heavy-ass baseball bag behind me that was full of our gloves, bats, and balls. I swear they made me the equipment manager just because they thought I'd get tired of dragging everyone's shit to and from the baseball diamond, but it didn't work. Even getting heckled for not being able to hit as hard, throw as far, or catch as good as them didn't work to drive me away. And my persistence paid off, because by the time I was a freshman in high school—their senior year—I joined the guys on the varsity baseball team, and we took the state title for the first time in fifteen years.

After brunch, we load up in an Uber and set off to our first stop; a baseball field that I rented out for us to have a friendly home-run derby competition with each other.

"Are you fucking serious!?" A grin splits Connor's face, and his eyes light up like a child on Christmas. "Dude, we've been talking about doing something like this for years."

"I pulled out all the stops for you, bro. They got bats, balls, gloves, and buckets of cold beer sitting on ice waiting for us. But just because it's your bachelor party, it doesn't mean I'm going to take it easy on you."

"Whoa, whoa, whoa! Are you forgetting who holds the record for the furthest home-run in Smoky Valley High history? Oh wait, that would be me."

I laugh. "Yeah, well, a foot further and I would have had you."

"Hey, it doesn't matter whether you win by

an inch or a mile. Winning is winning." He opens his arms wide in an attempt to sound like Dom from *The Fast and the Furious*.

"All right, settle down, Toretto," I say, slugging him on his shoulder.

We reach the field and meet with the representative to get checked in and grab the equipment we need for the three-hour time slot I reserved.

"Damn, this brings back some fucking memories, fellas," Lavelle says, squeezing both Connor and I's shoulders as we admire the well-kept baseball field.

He's not lying. Just one look at the dugout, and I can taste cherry Gatorade and sunflower seeds. I can smell pine-tar and freshly cut grass. I can hear the crack of the baseball coming off the bat and smack of the ball being caught in my glove. And I can picture a field full of my teammates and people in the stands cheering us on as we claw and fight our way through Saturday morning double-headers.

The grass is emerald green, the dirt is smoothed out perfectly, the chalk lines are freshly painted, and the sun is shining down on the field. And even though I've never been here before, it's all a familiar scene that sparks up nostalgia.

After the home-run derby, we gather on the bleachers to shotgun beers and reminisce about our state championship run before grabbing another Uber to take us back to Enchanted Shores so we can shower and get ready for stop number two.

I step out of the shower and wrap my towel around my waist. Water drips from the ends of my hair down to my chest as I grab my phone to call Kasie. I wish I could say it's to see how the bachelorette party is going——especially since she's meeting Olivia today——but really, it's simply because I miss her. I haven't heard her bubbly voice in too long.

"Hey, loser!" she exclaims as she picks up my call and my heart. "What's up?"

"Nothing, just wanted to check up on you."

Wow, that came out clingy as fuck.

"Oh, hold on, okay?" I hear her set the phone down and, in the background, I can hear her laughing and then, in unison, I hear the girls say "Cheers!" I listen to the sound of their clinking glasses, and my heart starts to race as I wait for her to pick the phone back up. The seconds pass like hours before she finally comes back on the phone. "I'm back. Sorry, we were taking a group shot. So, what's up? How's the bachelor party going?"

"It's going great. The custom bobbleheads were a hit—thanks for helping me find a shop that makes them by the way—Connor has been cheesing all day, and I won the home-run derby, so I'd say it's been pretty successful so far."

"Wow, you actually won something?"

I scoff. "Is me winning really that surprising?"

"Well, yeah, I mean, I *always* beat you."

"Wait, what do you mean you *always* beat me? Have I been present for these beatings?"

"Oh, you have. And I've got the pictures to prove it. Remember Dave & Busters a couple weeks ago when I beat you in that basketball shootout game?"

"The one where you Snapchatted our score and then made me take my 'loser' shot of tequila for the world to see?"

"Yep, that's the one."

"No recollection whatsoever," I say with a prankish tone.

She chuckles. "Oh, whatever. Anyways, hey, I got to go. The male strippers are here."

"Strippers?" My eyes widen and my tone sounds more jealous than I intend for it to. Hopefully she doesn't notice.

Kasie bursts into laughter. "I'm totally kidding. But I *do* have to go. The girls want to go dance, and they're looking at me like they're going to throw me overboard if I don't get off the phone, so..."

"All right, yeah, I'll talk to you later. Have fun, Kase."

"You too," she says, and then before she hangs up, I hear her playfully whine to the group,

"Okay, I'm coming, I'm coming."

I smile to myself and watch her smiling contact picture disappear from my phone screen and with it, my heart squeezes once more. Between hanging out with Nate and Connor the other day, and then Kasie being gone the whole next day, and then today being the bachelor party, I feel like it's been forever since I got to enjoy her company. I'm longing for it so much I can hardly stand it.

Damn, why is missing you so hard today?

I take a seat in one of the dining chairs, bury my face in my hands, and groan aloud because my mind is in a Kasie-filled haze.

I'm not going to be able to bury these feelings, am I?

A pounding at my door interrupts my moment, and I can hear the guys heckling me from the hallway.

I open the door, and Nate sighs heavily as the guys come in with a case of beer. "See, I told you his ass wouldn't be ready to go yet. Man, I bet Kasie takes quicker showers than you."

I don't even notice that I don't react to the

lighthearted jab until Connor wraps his arm around my shoulder and says, "Damn, you're going to let him get away with that shit, bro? You good?"

I laugh softly, and Lavelle is the first to notice something is off because he says, "Oh, I know what that look means."

"What are you talking about?" I look at him like he's crazy, trying to brush him off like I'm not in desperate need of advice that I can't get because of my charade. The guys all stare at me, waiting for some revelation, but even if I wanted to come clean, this is Connor's day and I don't want to take the spotlight, especially if he doesn't take kindly to me lying. "I'm fine, guys. I'm just trying to decide on my outfit, and I didn't realize you guys were coming over. And by the way, Kasie does not take quicker showers than me." I give Nate a contemptuous look.

Lavelle narrows his eyes like he knows I'm lying, but he doesn't push. "All right, bruh, well, hurry up and get changed into your *outfit*, so we can hit the next spot."

Chapter Fifteen

Kasie

It's official, Olivia is so sweet…and quiet. She's also gorgeous! Her light brown skin is flawless, she's got a perfect, dimpled smile, and her doe-eyes make her look like she can do no wrong. I haven't had much time to talk to her yet, although I've been trying to include her in conversations and stuff, but she's definitely someone who sits back and takes everything in, only talking when she truly has something to say.

After dancing and taking a round of shots, Mila decides it's time to jump off the back deck of the yacht and into the ocean, which is exciting because it's so hot today and the turquoise water is as tempting as it is beautiful.

One after the other, the girls jump in, until

it's Olivia's turn. I glance at her, waiting for her to jump, and then I see it—she's terrified. She leans over the edge to look down into the ocean and then jumps back.

"I can't do it," she says quickly. "I can't do it. Look at this, I'm shaking," she says, showing me her hands that are in fact trembling. "Ugh, I thought I could push myself, but I can't."

"Well, what if we jump together?" I ask, offering my hand and a friendly smile. She looks over the edge again, and I can see it in her eyes; she wants to, but she's still scared. So I encourage her again. "Girl, you've got this," and then I make another motion for her to grab my hand.

After a few seconds, she grabs my hand, and, together, we inch closer to the edge. "What if there's a shark down there? Or an octopus, or a giant jellyfish?"

"Or just a good time with friends. Come on, on the count of three, we jump. Deal?"

She threads her hand through her long, black curls and takes a deep breath. "Okay, let's do this, before I change my mind."

I nod as I start counting down, and on three,

we leave the deck together and splash into the ocean.

Hours later...

We're outside of the resort nightclub, waiting on Penelope to finish smoking, when some creepy, drunk guy in a muscle tank and backward hat comes up to her and asks, "Do you want to wrap those lips around me next? I guarantee I taste better."

"Um, no," Penelope responds, frowning.

"Ahh, come on, sexy," he says, adjusting his hat and stepping further into her bubble space. He's not very tall, but he's still much bigger than all of us. "Give me one good reason, and I'll leave you alone," he slurs with his hooded eyes glazed over.

"Because no is a complete sentence," I snap, recalling my dad's voice drilling that lesson into my head all throughout my childhood. I don't mean to answer for her, but I can't stand people—especially guys—who think the word *no* should come with an explanation.

He turns my way and stares daggers straight into my soul. "You got a mouth on you. What about you? Are you trying to get dicked down tonight?"

"Yes," I say matter of factly, "but not by you, so why don't you just go back inside and leave us alone?"

"That's too bad because you got them fuck me eyes. You couldn't handle this anyway. I'd stretch you out."

Olivia choke-laughs on her drink and the asshole turns to her next. I begin to ball my fist up, ready to spring into action if I need to.

"What the hell is so funny?" he snarls, and his companion finally notices the commotion and steps in.

"Dude, come on, you're drunk. Let's just get back inside," his friend says.

"No, fuck that. I want to know what this bitch is laughing at."

"Okay, first off," Olivia says, in full defense mode, and I'm loving this girl more by the second. "Literally learn how to talk to a woman if you *ever* expect to get laid. And second, her vagina could push out a whole-ass baby and it would go back to normal, so I'm pretty sure your little four-inch cock isn't going to be what does her in."

All of us girls burst into laughter and rally around Olivia as the guy's friend pulls him away and they head back inside.

"Wow, sis," Penelope says, looking at Olivia like she's a completely different person. "I did not expect all of that to come from your mouth. I'm impressed."

"Yes, thank you for standing up for me," I say.

"I have no idea where that came from," Olivia says with wide eyes. "But it was liberating…and scary. I guess I'm doing all types of things that scare me today."

We all laugh again and then get ready to head back inside. Olivia taps me on the shoulder and asks to talk with me, so she and I stay outside as the rest of the girls head back in.

Olivia brushes strands of hair away from her face. "I wanted to thank you again…for the yacht earlier."

"Of course. I'm happy you jumped."

"I am too. Don't get me wrong, I'm not signing up to do it again anytime soon, but I'm really glad I did. I feel this odd sense of accomplishment. And honestly, considering who I am to Donnie, I'm surprised you even cared enough to help me." She looks at the ground.

"If I'm being honest, I thought I was going to really, really dislike you—"

"At least you didn't expect to hate me, I guess." She laughs nervously.

"Hate's a strong word. But you're definitely not what I expected…in a good way, of course."

"I'm happy to hear that. And I swear, I'm not here to cause problems for you and Donnie. I'm actually happy to hear he's dating again," she says. I narrow my eyes, wondering how she knows he wasn't dating, because I know he hasn't told her. She must notice my piqued curiosity because she quickly says, "Grapevine. It's a small town."

"I get it. So, if you don't mind me asking—
no judgment—but why the last-minute decision to
come to the wedding?" I ask, and she gives me the
same curious look I gave her a second ago.
"Grapevine," I say with a chuckle.

She inspects her fingernails and then sighs.
"The sad and probably selfish truth is, I needed to
see with my own eyes that he's happy. I know it's
been three years, but I really do care about him. We
were childhood friends, and ending things the way
that I did, I've grown to regret it. And believe me, I
know it sounds like I'm not over him, but I am. I
just want him to be happy. You are super outgoing
and nice, so it's not hard to imagine that he is. But
with your blessing, I hoped that I could maybe talk
to him and apologize for hurting him the way I did."

As flattering as her compliment is, an alarm
sounds in my head. I have to take this girl at her
word, and while she seems sweeter than sugar, I
don't really know her well enough to
wholeheartedly trust her. But as much as she seems
to need some form of closure with him, I know he
needs it too, so, reluctantly, I give her my blessing
and hope I don't regret it.

After the nightclub, Penelope leads Olivia back to her room to take care of her because she is throwing up from too many shots. Poor girl was so nervous to see Donnie tonight that she was throwing back shots like *she* was the bride-to-be.

We make it to the cute little speakeasy lounge, where the guys are already hanging out in the VIP section. Donnie is all smiles and looking as handsome as can be in his dress pants, button-up shirt, and vest that perfectly accents his athletic torso. I'm happy to see him—like ecstatic, because I've missed him so much all day—but at the same time it *is* a little bittersweet.

Earlier I came to terms with my feelings for Donnie. Morgan says I should tell him. Damen says I should tell him. Everything in me says I should tell him. So, I will. I just don't know when. I feel like telling him now just means I'm trying to force something to happen that's not supposed to right now. There's a reason things didn't line up for us the other night. I may not know what that reason is, but right now just isn't our time. So, I've decided I'm going to hold these feelings in and revisit them at a later date. If we're both still single and it feels like the right time again, I'll go for it. Until then, that handsome guy over there in the VIP section, double-fisting his drinks—I swear if one of those is mine, I'll collapse in his arms—that's my best friend, and no one can take that from us.

Chapter Sixteen

Donnie

"There she is," I say, greeting Kasie with a hug when she comes walking up the VIP section with the other girls—minus Olivia and Penelope, who I'm told are back in Olivia's room since she got pretty drunk earlier.

I'm not going to lie; I'm a little relieved that I didn't have to see her tonight. Surprisingly, I'd rather be sober when I see her.

"Aw, this is for me?" Kasie asks, looking like she could cry when I hand her the second drink I'm holding. "Yeah, I know how much you like Manhattans, so I figured I'd have one waiting for you. And this is a fancy one because it's smoked."

She accepts the drink and then pulls me down for a passionate kiss, massaging my tongue with hers. When I feel her seemingly pulling away to end the kiss, I move my hands to her cheeks, keeping her mouth connected to mine.

Stay, please. Just stay.

And she does until we back into the table and laugh when we almost knock our drinks over. She's got this sweet look that thrills me.

"Do you want to dance?" I ask when the acoustic band plays a slow song that we recognize.

"Right now? But there's no one out there right now. It would be just us."

I shrug my shoulders. "What's wrong with that?"

"Nothing, I'm just surprised, I guess. You must be pretty drunk if you're okay with taking me to dance to a slow song…just the two of us…with no one else out there…where everyone in the bar can see." She giggles.

"Ok, if you don't want to…" I grab my drink off the table and turn away from her.

"Hey!" she exclaims, grabbing my arm to turn me back around, and even though I knew she'd be smiling, I didn't expect that she'd be smiling so pretty. "Of course, I want to."

I grab her hand, and we stand in the middle

of an empty dance floor, swaying back and forth. I hate that she probably thinks this is just to keep up appearances, but it's not. Bringing her out here, away from the group who's getting a little too rowdy for this quiet-ish lounge, it was just so I could hold her close, so I could pretend for just a little while longer that I've got exactly what I want. So I could do my best to commit to memory how wonderful this feels to hold her in my arms while her head is pressed against my chest.

But eventually, it's time to move on. The group is loud and ready to hit the pool bar, so we all join together for the walk over. Kasie and I are holding hands, walking together until Celeste—one of the other bridesmaids who Kasie said she hit it off with—pulls her forward to walk with her and Mila, citing that I can have Kasie anytime since she's my girlfriend while they only have a few days to kick it.

Oh, how I wish you were right, Celeste.

One by one, the bachelor/bachelorette party decreases in number. Connor and Mila's drunk asses snuck back to their room about thirty minutes ago. Nate hit it off with some girl earlier, and assuming she doesn't have a boyfriend or husband out here that we'll have to protect him from, he's probably getting lucky. Marcus and Gavin are doing their best taking turns complimenting Emily, one of the other bridesmaids, and Lavelle and I are hanging around the bar area, watching Kasie, Celeste, and another bridesmaid in the middle of the crowded dance floor, dancing the night away.

"She's mesmerizing," I say to Lavelle, nudging his elbow as I point towards Kasie.

Ever since we met up with the girls, I've been starstruck over her, wracking my brain, wondering what it would be like if we weren't pretending. Everything in me says *just fucking tell her how you feel*, but then that little voice of reason kicks in and reminds me of what I'm risking if I were to tell her. I'm terrified to be the reason our friendship falls apart.

Why can't I just be fine with leaving well enough alone? Why am I so intent on ruining our friendship just so we can maybe be lovers?

"Yeah, you're a lucky man."

I sigh heavily and take a swig of my beer. "Everyone keeps saying that, bro, but I'm not," I tell him, not even realizing I'm about to come clean. "She's not really my girlfriend. I made it up so that my mom wouldn't keep trying to talk to me about getting back on the dating wagon."

Lavelle scoffs and looks at me like he's waiting for the punch line, but when it doesn't come, he widens his eyes. "Oh, you're serious? Fuck, you know that never ends well, right?" His tone is more enthused than it should be.

"Tell me about it." I scratch the back of my neck and sigh. "Two weeks without catching feelings, that's all I had to do. I mean, damn, we've known each other for two years, and I never caught relationship-type feelings. Convincing her to be my fake girlfriend was supposed to be the safe option, but in less than two weeks, my head is as hazy as those IPAs you like to drink."

"Hazy for what? You're falling for your best friend, that's fucking awesome, bruh. I'm not seeing a problem here."

"The problem is she's my best friend. I'm

not supposed to want any more than that. But the other day, something changed, and now when I hear that beautiful belly laugh of hers, I get chills up my spine, and when she looks at me, I feel like it's just me and her against the world. And I feel like I'm going crazy because I swear, she's been giving me these sweet looks and then these longing stares, like I'm really starting to wonder if she's feeling me, too, or am I just wishful thinking and seeing things I want to see?"

"All right, first of all, take another big gulp of your beer and relax, bruh," he instructs, and I listen. "Second, you just need to be up front with her. Nothing good ever comes from hiding the way you're feeling. What's the worst that happens?"

I scoff. "What's the worst that happens? I'll tell you. I confuse the shit out of her, because I've sworn up and down that I'm not blurring lines, when in reality, I must need glasses or something, because I didn't even see when the lines started blurring. Fuck, I don't even know if they exist anymore."

"No, the worst that can happen is you holding onto those feelings, never confessing, and living with regret. Don't wait until it's too late to tell her."

"I don't know, man. We just had our first fight last night, and this morning we finally kind of sort of made up, so the timing just sucks."

"Fuck timing. Nothing ever lines up perfectly. If you wait for things to do that, all you'll do is wait. Life is messy and unpredictable, and just when you think you've got it all figured out, fuck a curve ball; life throws you a damn knuckleball. But it doesn't matter, because when you find a heart worth going through all of life's messes with, that's beautiful. And maybe it's her or maybe it's not."

"What happens if it's not? There is no one else like her, I'm sure of it. I can't lose her, Velle."

"Losing is a part of life, man. If you never lost anything, you'd never know how to appreciate what you have…or had. You know Rachelle and I are getting a divorce?"

"Oh, damn, I'm sorry, bro. I didn't know."

"It's all good. We've kept it quiet, but yeah, it hurts. We had a lot a good times together, she and I. But at some point, I got used to having her around. I got complacent. I stopped doing the little things that made her feel appreciated. And then I got used to that and stopped doing the bigger things, too. By the time I realized it, she had one foot out the door. I'm at peace with it, though. Do I wish I could go back and do things differently? Yeah, of course, I do. But I can't, so there's no sense in dwelling on the past.

I know Olivia hurt you, but she's your past, and it's time you leave her there. I don't know much about Kasie, but from the outside looking in, you two have a good thing, so don't waste it worrying about shit you can't control. A'ight?"

Well, that was like a fastball to the face. He's not lying, though.

"Yeah, you know what? You're right. I want to tell her, even if that means she doesn't reciprocate the feelings. I just hope if she doesn't, that we'll find a way to get through it."

"This isn't high school. We're all adults now, so you will. And I hope you get you want, D. You're a good dude, and you deserve to find someone who makes your hopeless romantic heart beat again." He laughs, shoving me a little as he takes a drink of his beer.

Gavin approaches us and leans drunkenly on

Lavelle and I's shoulders. "Hey, I don't mean to break up whatever this sweet little moment is, but I just seen Kasie at the bar smiling and laughing with some tattooed guy, and when he walked off towards the resort, she followed. I don't want to jump to conclusions, but it looked sus, I'm not going to lie."

"That's my cue. I'll catch up with you guys later." I clap his shoulder and nod at Lavelle before leaving the pool bar area, heading back toward the resort in search of Kasie. I call her phone a couple of times and it goes straight to voicemail, which is weird, because that doesn't usually happen. I hurry down the maze of hallways, trying not to worry. I reach our room door, open it, and my heart sinks when I see Kasie's heels kicked off against the wall and the strap of her sparkly, black dress she was wearing peeking out from underneath our half-shut bedroom door.

Chapter Seventeen

Kasie

I was doing good for the better part of the day, but something about the night sky and all the stars twinkling down at me tonight just makes me kind of sad again. I don't know, it feels bigger and kind of makes me feel lonely. I wanted to stay and hang out with the girls a little longer, but I'm just ready to be by myself for a little while. I even ignored Donnie's calls. I'm sure he's wondering where I'm at, so he can keep sweeping me off my feet, but I'm done with pretending for the night. So, I'm stripped out of my pretty dress and put on his big, comfy T-shirt and pajama shorts, I've got my second glass of wine in my hands, and I've got the evening sea breeze playing with my messy bun as I sit in the patio chair next to the infinity pool. I've also got the playlist Donnie sent me yesterday playing, and it makes me seriously miss him.

Ugh, you would think he's been gone for months the way my heart hurts.

I start scrolling through pictures of Donnie and I from this vacation and smile at the memories that feel like forever ago already. The sound of the sliding glass door opening behind me startles me, and I turn around in my seat. My heart flutters as a small smile plays on my lips.

There's Donnie. His hair is a little messier than it was when I saw him at the beach bar earlier.

"Can we talk?" he asks.

I don't like the sound of that.

"Of course, but can I say something first?" I ask, and he nods. I stand up from the chair and pull myself together. "I'm sorry I stayed mad at you for so long. I know you didn't mean to stand me up. I may have overreacted a little."

"Hey," he says, coming closer and bringing me into his arms, which is comforting and unexpected. *I guess maybe I look sadder than I think?* "You don't have anything to be sorry for. I was an asshole, and you reacted exactly the way you should have."

"I just want things to be normal between us again," I say, looking up at him, studying his face like he's hiding clues about what he came to discuss. And how he even knew I was here is puzzling, but I don't care about that right now; I'm just glad he's here.

"About that… Kasie, I don't think things can go back to the way they were."

My heart sinks. "It was just one fight, Donnie. I'm sure we can get past it." I chuckle nervously.

He smiles gently, looking deep into my soul for what feels like forever. I'm tempted to tell him to just come out with it. But instead, I just stare back, blinking sweetly as I wait for him to say something…*anything*.

"This past week and a half has opened my eyes and made me realize that I want to start dating again."

He looks away from me like he can barely stand to tell me.

"That's great," I say halfheartedly, because it's really not. I feel horribly selfish for thinking it, but I'm barely ready to accept my failed attempt at telling him I have feelings for him, let alone ready to accept that he's going to be looking for someone who isn't me.

"Yeah, I hope so. You know, when I asked you to be my fake girlfriend, I never expected for this to happen, and I swear I didn't mean for it to, I don't even know how or when it happened—"

"Donnie, you don't need my permission to date, it's okay."

"I actually do need your permission for this. Just listen." He takes a deep, shaky breath. "Waking up to your smile every morning—okay, more like you jumping on top of me, but hey, you still have a smile on your face, so it counts," he says with a smirk that makes me laugh softly. "And falling asleep with you each night, having you next to me during family lunches and dinners, all this romantic boyfriend-girlfriend stuff that we're doing, I don't want to do these things with anyone else."

Oh my gosh.

I cover a gasp with my hands, and my eyes well up with tears that sit in the corners of my eyes as he continues. "I know it probably comes as a surprise, and like I said, I swear falling for you wasn't the plan, but, Kasie—I think about you when I shouldn't. I'm feeling things I said I wasn't, and I have to admit that I stopped trying to keep up appearances days ago. All these romantic gestures have been just to see you smile and to make you feel special, because you are the most important person in my life."

His rough hand cups mine and a tear escapes and slides down my cheek. He captures it with his unoccupied thumb and looks me in the eyes. "Kasie, I came here to ask if you will you take a chance with me and be my girlfriend, and not just best friend?"

I barely let the words finish leaving his lips before I push up on my tiptoes and answer his question with a desperate kiss that begs him to take care of my heart, because he's not just another guy I'll be dating. He's Donnie Joseph Walker: my best friend, my sunshine, my everything and now—I can't believe I'm really going to say this—my boyfriend.

The way he draws me closer as our lips cling together, it just feels right, and I hope with every piece of me that it is. And I also want him to know something else, so when my lips part from his, and he stares into my eyes with a smile that you'd expect from someone who just found what they'd been searching their life for, I smack his muscular arm and let my reciprocating smile slip off my face and turn to a contemptuous, sulky look.

"Ouch, what was that for?" he asks, looking confused and a little amused.

"For the record, I was going to confess my feelings for you during our sushi date that I got ghosted at."

His jaw drops, and the surprise on his face—and in his eyes—is all I needed to make the admission worth it.

"Ohhhh. Wow, that puts a lot of things into perspective."

"Mmhmm. You know, now that we're dating, if you ever ghost me like that again, you won't get me walking around in sexy underwear when…no, not when, *if* you wake up," I say, folding my arms across my chest now and trying hard to keep my resting bitch face. Still, it softens when I see the tender way he's looking at me. He gently brings me back into his arms until I'm pressed against his firm chest. He holds me tight, like he's trying to make certain nothing can push us apart this time. No pushy waves, no unexpected eighty-mile-per-hour wind gusts, nothing can take me from him in this moment.

After a moment, he whispers in my ear, and goosebumps flood my warm body at the rumble of his deep voice. "It won't ever happen again, you have my word." He presses his lips to my cheek, and for a second, I feel him start toward my neck but then he stops and pulls away. "Wait a minute," he says, narrowing his eyes. "There was a purpose to wearing that sexy underwear?"

I throw a look of feigned innocence on my face while I answer his question. "I might have been trying to get a rise out of you."

"Oh, you got a *rise* out of me all right."

"Donnie!" I exclaim, widening my eyes. My cheeks turn a few degrees warmer than the rest of my body as I draw my bottom lip between my teeth.

"What? You know you're sexy." He leans back in and brushes his lips against my neck, and my heart pounds as I wait for his next move.

I gasp quietly as it comes in the form of his tongue snaking up my neck then grabbing hold of my ear lobe with his teeth before returning to my neck.

"It's not fair," I say, biting my lip to stop a quiet moan from escaping as he spends time kissing my sweet spot—my neck. "It's like…" I pause, my breath growing heavier as I'm unable to hold the moan back any longer. "It's like you have the other team's playbook, and you know exactly what plays to call," I say quickly before another moan can interrupt me.

It's true, though. I can't count the number of conversations we've had where I've detailed my sex life to him, telling him things I like and things I don't. Donnie's mentioned a few things here and there that he likes, but, ugh, why did I let him skimp on the details? He's my best friend, and I feel like when it comes to sex, I'm in the dark.

What if he hates sex with me? I hadn't even considered the possibility.

Now my heart is pounding harder, and not just because he's walking me back against the patio wall.

He must sense my hesitation, because he stops kissing me and asks, "Are you okay?"

I stare back at his pretty eyes that seem even more mesmerizing under the stars tonight. "I'm a little nervous."

"If you're not ready, we can stop."

"No, I want this. I just want our first time to be perfect, and I don't know what you like. And I feel like you know everything about me. And—"

He caresses my cheek with his rough palm, and it stops my thought. "I'm nervous, too. But you know what? Perfection is overrated. I just want you to feel the same way you made me feel from the moment you jumped on my bed to wake me up two years ago."

"Annoyed?"

He chuckles lightly. "Like nothing will ever be the same again…in a good way, obviously."

"It really won't, will it?"

This is terrifying, thrilling, and super exciting all at the same time.

He shakes his head and then asks, "Are you ready?"

"For us or for sex?"

"Both," he smirks, and I feel a tingle between my legs.

Perfect may be overrated, but when he lifts me into his arms, and I yelp, wrapping my legs around his rugged torso, everything we do after is our version of perfect. We don't make it to the room before we're at each other's lips. We bump into the bedroom doorframe and mix laughter and groans of pain. Once he places me on the bed, we can't get each other's clothes off fast enough.

And when I'm lying there, completely naked and vulnerable, waiting for his next move, I'm covered with comfort as he kisses down my chest and stomach, taking care when it comes to fingering and licking my clit. And when he makes me come against his mouth, he doesn't fill me with his big, hard cock just to get his. No, while he's inside me, steadily pounding my pussy, he takes his time— kissing me, kissing my neck, kissing my shoulders, flipping me over and kissing my shoulder blades, stroking me with his cock until my moans are so loud that I swear our room neighbors can hear me.

It's so good that I flip over, push him to his back, and ride him as he pinches my nipples and massages my clit. And then he places his hands on my hips and grabs my ass while I ride him and control the motion. I can tell he feels good, because he's breathing deeply and his pupils are blown wide. When I pick up the pace, arching my back to hit the spot even better, he buries his hand in my hair and tugs, and I swear, this is what making love feels like.

After I come on his hard cock, he lifts me off him, lays me back on the bed, lifts my legs up over his shoulders and fills me up again, kissing my ankles and whispering beautifully filthy things until he comes inside me, his steady grunts and moans finally quieting as we both lay our backs on the bed.

I turn to my side, shoving my messy hair back away from my face, catching my breath as I stare at the man who just found another way to take my breath away. I admire his toned muscles and abs before he turns to his side and smiles at me, leaning over to kiss my forehead before I surrender into his arms.

I'm taking an after-sex shower, washing up and taking my time as I reminisce already about the captivating pleasure I just felt. Before I came in here to shower, I gave Donnie a sexual hint, hoping he'll join me, and after another minute goes by, I hear the door open, and my pulse races the smile that immediately forms on my lips.

He pops his head in with a flirty grin, and I ask innocently, "What are you doing?"

"I figured we could wash up together. What do you think?"

I think I suggested that without suggesting it.

"Come here," I say, curving my index finger in a come-hither motion.

When he does, I wrap my arms around his neck, kissing him while the water drenches our bodies. I slip my tongue inside his mouth and massage his tongue with mine before he begins to lower himself, and immediately, my core begins to literally weep for another round.

He grabs my ass and pulls my pussy to his mouth, licking and extracting moans from me as the shower water drenches his strong back and shoulders.

"You're…" I pause, breathing heavily as I try to focus on finishing my sentence, "going to drown yourself. Oh my gosh!" I exclaim, my eyes rolling back while the pleasure pulsing through my body causes another moan to cry out. "Fuck me, Donnie."

And he does. He gets to his feet and I look up at him, biting down on my lip. I turn around and he kisses down my neck to the tattoo on my shoulder before bending me over. My hands are against the shower wall as his big cock slides inside me. The water pours down on us as he crowds me against the cold tile until finally, we both come again.

Chapter Eighteen

Donnie

~ Day 12, Thursday ~

On cloud nine, euphoric, a feeling of ecstasy, intoxicated…all words that should accurately describe what's going on inside me right now; yet, somehow, all those words pale in comparison to how I'm really feeling.

There's an indescribable peace that comes from waking up this morning next to Kasie, feeling her soft breath against my bare chest while I play with her hair. It's not the stillness of the morning, not the sound of ocean waves just beyond our open patio doors, not even the aroma of hot coffee being poured out of the machine. It's the promise of a life with the girl who has filled my heart up from day one, the girl I never saw coming.

"Are you sure this is what you want?" Kasie's tired voice rasps. "You weren't just drunk or feeling some type of way because your brother's wedding is a couple days away?"

She lifts her head from my chest and moves to a cross-legged position beside me, watching my eyes as if she wants to make sure they're truthful.

I reach for her hand, and she allows me to hold it in mine. "I wasn't drunk. I remember everything I said, everything we did, and I meant it all. What about you? Are you having second thoughts?"

She shakes her head, and a knock at our door turns both our heads in that direction. I get up to check the peephole, to see who would show up so early. Granted, it's ten o'clock in the morning, but there's nothing planned, aside from our mid-afternoon parasailing and hotel room sushi date.

I frown as my nerves jump and my heart thumps quicker at who I see. "It's Olivia," I whisper to Kasie, who followed me out with a blanket wrapped around her body.

What is she doing here?

Olivia looks just the same as she did three years ago, except maybe a little more confident.

"Oh, yeah, I'm sorry. I forgot. She asked if I

would allow her to talk to you and apologize or something. I was going to tell you last night but then we…you know."

I chuckle softly, feeling my cheeks heat up a little and hers turn pinker than they were a second ago too. I guess this is still pretty new and kind of crazy—the good kind. "It's okay, I prefer what we did last night."

She bites her lip and smiles a little. "Go ahead and let her in, I'll just be in the room. But you better cover all that up." She looks at me sternly, making a circular gesture in the air around my chest and abs.

I take a deep breath that doesn't calm my nerves like I hoped it would and then open the door.

I stand there, awkwardly silent, and so does Olivia, until she mutters quietly, "H-Hey." She lifts her hand in greeting, and I think I wear a small smile, speechless for a couple more seconds. Her long, curly hair is draped over her shoulders, and her bright red lipstick is smeared over her plump lips. She's wearing the same pair of glasses she had on the day I left. It's like a fucking ghost of my past is staring at me right now, yet she's not a ghost— she's really here.

"Umm, c-come in." I open the door wider, and she steps in as I shut the door behind her. "I'm going to grab a shirt—"

"Here you go." Kasie appears at the bedroom doorframe, dressed in a tank top and sweatpants. She tosses me the shirt, and I see a little hint of possessiveness in her eyes; it makes me chuckle to myself.

"Thanks, Kase," I say, catching the shirt and sliding it on.

She smiles, shoving her messy hair away from her face and tossing it to one side before greeting Olivia, "Hey, girl. How are you feeling?"

"I had a morning jog, so I'm much more alive than I was earlier this morning. I'm pretty sure I've already had enough water to satisfy my daily intake." Olivia laughs nervously. "I know jogging with a hangover sounds insane, but Donnie dragged me with him back in the day, and surprisingly, it wasn't as bad as I thought it would be."

Olivia smiles at me and then looks away to the ground.

I chuckle softly, recalling the memory of that morning. Olivia had been at the movies with some friends before meeting up with me and the rest of our crew at a house party. She was determined to get on our level, so she shot Fireball whiskey back like there was going to be a shortage—and severely regretted it the next morning. I was pretty hungover too, so I made us a protein shake and suggested a jog. She hated the idea—as much as everyone else who I've ever suggested the idea to—until we got back from that jog. All the nutrients from the protein shake, the waters we took with us, and the vitamin D—the real kind—worked together to change her life. From that moment, she was hooked on morning hangover jogs. She even dragged *me* out a handful of times, because I'm not *always* down for running when I feel like shit.

Kasie chuckles lightly, and the vibe is just awkward right now. I don't know if it's because Kasie and I just made it official, and now I've got my first love standing in our living room, dressed up like she's going to a fancy brunch while Kasie and I are dressed like we just woke up from a bachelor/bachelorette party with the crazy hair to match, or if it's because Kasie and I were kind of in the middle of an important conversation, or simply because of the way things left off with Olivia and me.

We're all just standing there, silent and seemingly waiting on a pin to drop when I cut into the silence. "So, umm, why don't we go to the patio, so we can chat."

Olivia nods. "Bye, Kasie." She gives a passing glance at Kasie, giving a small wave that Kasie reciprocates, although she looks like she's on a completely different island right now.

"You look good," Olivia says as she takes her seat, and then quickly backtracks. "I mean, I didn't...t-that's not how I wanted that to come out——"

"You look good, too, Olivia," I say, trying to relieve this unspoken tension, but saying her name out loud, it leaves me with this empty feeling that I can't really explain. For a long time, I wondered if I'd ever see her again. If I'd ever get the chance to understand what happened between us. Honestly, even though I was nervous a few days ago when

Kasie and I talked about me getting closure, now I'm just ready to put her in my past. It feels cold saying it like that, because I grew up with her and I do care for her, just not in the way I used to.

"I'm sorry, I had this whole speech thought out in my head, but it's just a jumbled mess up there right now…" She clears her throat and then asks, "Umm, so, how are you? How's life?" She stares at me with those big brown doe-eyes that used to make me melt.

I shrug. "Life's good. I'm working on this pretty big project right now with a glass staircase and an underground theatre. It's pretty cool. I've been documenting it on Instagram." I pull my phone out to show her a quick video. She leans in closer, and a familiar fruity scent wafts under my nose as the video plays. When the video is over, I lean back to my side of the table. "What about you, how's life?"

"Good. I, umm…I'm studying to be a nurse."

"Congratulations."

"Thank you." She forces a smile—I can't believe I still know what it looks like when her smile is forced. We sit in silence for what feels like at least a couple minutes before she says, "Okay, so I'm just going to cut to the chase… I was wrong for the way I broke things off between us and I want you to know that I'm sorry. When you told me you wanted to move clear across the country to California, I freaked out inside, and I should have told you how I was feeling instead of just going along with it," she says, looking at the ground.

When I start to respond, she looks back up at me and cuts me off. "Please let me finish. I've wanted to say this for so long. Three years ago, you asked me when it was over for me, and the truth is, I didn't even know I was going to go through with it until I started saying the words. And I'm not here to make amends, cause problems for you and Kasie, or win you back or anything like that. I just…I need you to know that I regret leaving you, Donnie. If I could go back and take the risk with you, in a heartbeat, I would. But that opportunity is gone. You're happy, and Kasie is so perfect for you. She's pretty, funny, adventurous… And sweet, just like you. I hope she knows what she has, and I pray she treats you better than I did. Again, I am so sorry, and I hope you can forgive me. At the very least, just please don't hate me."

Wow, just…wow. So many emotions flowing through my body right now. I run my hand down my face, sighing. "Olivia, I don't hate you. I was upset, of course, angry even. But I never hated you. I understand now that it was a big ask, and I should have considered how you felt more than what I did. I was so wrapped up in planning our future that I forgot to live our present, and worse, I neglected to check up on you before making those huge decisions. I'm sorry for that."

"It's okay, we both made mistakes… Can I ask you something though? Why didn't you come back?"

Damn, I'm like a deer in headlights to *that* question. I sit and think, hoping I can come up with a reasonable explanation but all I come up with is, "I don't know. Pride, I guess? I felt betrayed by someone I'd grown up so close with. Coping with that was hard because we were friends first, so it was a different kind of heartbreak, you know? Which is why—" I stop, realizing I might be spilling too much, and I don't want to make this more awkward or make her feel bad. "Never mind."

"Which is why what?"

Fuck it, just say it. I'm tired of holding

things in.

"Why I was worried about Kasie and I being together…because of what happened to me and you. Kasie and I were best friends first. I don't want what happened to us to happen with me and her. If I lost her the way I lost you, it might literally kill me."

"Well, it doesn't take a rocket scientist to see that she's head over heels for you. And it would seem that you are head over heels for her too. Just…when things get hard and it's not all sunshine and rainbows, don't give up on each other. That's how you don't end up like us."

I nod. "Thank you. And I forgive you, by the way." I tip my lips into a smile, and she returns one back at me. "Friends?" I stick my hand out.

With tears in her eyes, she accepts my handshake, sniffling and wiping her eyes with her free hand. "Friends. And I forgive you too."

After we shake hands and stand to our feet, we embrace, and it feels like a weight has just been lifted off my chest. I didn't realize how much I needed this conversation. And now that I've had it, I feel even more confident that I'm ready for a relationship—a relationship with my best friend, Kasie.

I shut the door behind Olivia as she leaves and turn around to see Kasie standing at the bedroom doorway. "So, how'd it go?" she asks, inspecting her fingernails, and I can hear the jealousy in her tone which, honestly, is kind of cute on her.

"Kasie Pearce, are you jealous right now?" I ask, trying not look too amused while walking toward her. She looks at me with contempt, nibbling the inside corner of her bottom lip.

"What? No." She looks away from me as I stop in front of her and wait for her to be honest with me. "Ugh," she huffs. "Okay, fine, maybe a little bit," she says, and I can tell—and hear—that it kills her to admit it. "I'm sorry, it's just that…she's still in love with you."

"I know."

"You know?"

"She told me—in her own way of dancing around it without actually saying the words, but I picked it up. You know that she admitted if she could go back and change what happened, she would?" I place my hands on Kasie's hips, staring at her pretty dark, brown eyes. "But you don't have anything to worry about, because like I said the other day, I'm not interested in rekindling anything with her. I got the closure I needed."

She forces a smile, and it makes me nervous. "You don't want to consider it at all?"

"Consider what?" I ask, creasing brows and narrowing my eyes.

"If she's genuinely willing to move to California now, you could have your first love back, Donnie. I don't know, maybe it's worth considering now that you're ready to date again."

"All right, where's this coming from?"

"I think I need a glass of wine for this." She moves past me, making a B-line to the wine dispenser and pouring herself a glass and then me one, after confirming I'll have one with her.

We sit at the dining table, and Kasie takes a gulp of wine. "It's just that…two weeks ago, dating was the last thing on your mind, and now, you're about to jump into a relationship with someone who is looking for happily ever after, someone who goes all in, every time, no matter how much it hurts if it doesn't work out. But unlike all the others, you're not just another guy to me, and I don't want to be just another girl to you. I'm scared that if you don't have a chance to play the field a little bit before finding something serious again—like it would be with me—you'll grow to resent me, and I'll turn into just another girl who was once in your lineup. And… I don't want to look at you the way Olivia does. The regret plastered all over her face at just the mention of your name; I don't want to feel that."

"Kasie," I say, pushing my wine glass to the side and taking her small, soft hand in mine. "If there is another girl in this world who can make me feel like you do, I don't ever plan to find out. This isn't a game to me; I don't need to play the field to know that it's you who I want. I stopped dating three years ago because I knew I wasn't ready to put my whole heart into a relationship again, and it would have been a disservice to me *and* whoever I was dating. But I found a girl who changed all that. A girl who makes me want to close my eyes, take off running, and jump off the cliff, trusting that the water she told me about is really there."

"Who is she? She sounds amazing," Kasie says softly, wearing a pretty smile at the corner of her lips.

"She is." I gently pull her my way, and she abandons her chair for my lap. I kiss her bare shoulder, where her loose t-shirt has slipped down, and look her in her worried eyes. "You're not just another girl, Kasie. You're *my* girl. I don't ever want that to be a question."

"Are you sure I'm not just the safest option right now?"

I chuckle. "Safest option? The first day I met you, we rode a zipline that I'm still convinced wasn't up to code, and since then I've swam with sharks, cave dived, bungee jumped, whitewater rafted—all your ideas by the way—and later today we're going parasailing. I don't think you qualify as safe."

She giggles, smacking my arm softly before she breathes a long, relieved sigh. "I'm sorry. I'm just…really happy. I keep thinking I'm going to wake up and all of this is going to be a dream. Will you let me pinch your ass to make sure I'm awake?"

She reaches down at my ass before I have a chance to answer, and I squirm away from her determined hand with her still sitting on my lap. "That's not even how it works, weirdo. You have to pinch yourself."

"Fine, can I have a kiss at least? I feel like I haven't kissed you all morning."

I answer with a lopsided grin, and she twists eagerly on my lap to face me, spreading her legs on either side of me and, fuck, my cock is tingling and hardening with excitement.

Kasie clasps her arms around my neck, resting her forearms on my shoulders, looking me right in the eyes with a smile that awakens a sanctuary of butterflies in my stomach.

"You are so beautiful."

We both lean in, our lips meeting in the middle for what I expect to be a quick kiss, but Kasie's got other plans as she takes my lips hostage, grinding her hips against my hard cock. I slide my tongue against hers, our kisses growing in hunger and her hips increasing in speed. She moans quietly and gasps when I slip my hands inside the back of her shirt to caress her silky skin.

She stops kissing my lips to trail her tongue from the base of my neck to my ear, gently blowing the area she licked. Chills shoot up my spine and the little hairs on the back of my neck stand up. I unhook her bra and start to lift her shirt over her head, but she grabs both my wrists to stop me.

"Follow me," she leans in and whispers seductively in my ear before leaving my lap and walking toward the bedroom without looking back at me.

Damn, she's driving me crazy.

I admire her perky ass in her short pajama shorts, almost forgetting to follow her.

When I get to the bedroom, Kasie grabs the ends of my shirt with each hand and lifts it off me. I toss it on the bedroom floor as she starts placing tender kisses to my pecs before lowering herself to her knees. She looks up at me, biting down on her lip as she grabs hold of the waistband on my sweatpants and boxers. She's got this confident, titillating look that I've never seen before, and it throws me; my heart speeds up along with my breath. My cock is begging for her, and I'm at her mercy, waiting for her next move, while she's happily teasing me by taking her time.

She begins sliding my pants down, peppering kisses on my lower abdominal muscles until my hard cock is free and at full strength in front of her face.

She takes it in her hands, and I grunt with a rush of pleasure as I feel her circle the tip with her tongue, looking up at me for just a brief second, like she wants to make sure I'm enjoying what she's doing—and I imagine she didn't even need the visual confirmation on my face.

She licks up and down the full length of my cock before wrapping her soft lips around it, sucking and going further with each mouth stroke. I fist her hair but let her control the motion, and damn is she good at that.

"Ah, fuck, Kasie," I say, grunting and inadvertently throwing my head back to look up at the ceiling while she keeps sucking me, taking me to the back of her throat over and over.

She licks up and down my shaft once more and then puts the whole thing back in her mouth again, and I look down just in time to see her hand slipping between her legs while she continues sucking me.

She moans, increasing the speed of both her mouth and fingers. I reach down to grab her shirt and pull it off her, unhooking her bra right after. It falls to the floor, and I use both hands to grab Kasie's boobs, squeezing and kneading until her eyes roll back and her mouth slows down to almost motionless.

I lift her up off the floor and toss her on the bed, sliding her pajama shorts off and then her panties.

You've got the prettiest pussy I've ever seen.

I climb up until I'm hovering above her and then I pin her arms back and look her in the eyes as I push inside of her. Her jaw drops and a loud moan escapes. I thrust into her wet, warm pussy, filling every inch of her with my cock and steadily increasing the speed, letting go of her arms so I can play with her clit.

"Flip me over and fuck me," she rasps as I thrust her a couple more times before following directions.

I flip her and pull her hair back before

entering her again, railing her pussy from behind as she clenches the sheets and screams with pleasure.

After a bit, I pull out, flip her on her back, spreading her legs on the bed. I slip two fingers inside her soft pussy and pleasure her clit before putting my cock back in. When I do, I pound her until she comes, and then shortly after, I do too.

Chapter Nineteen

Kasie

Okay, so parasailing was every bit as thrilling as I hoped it would be; it had me screaming almost as much as Donnie did this morning. And oh my gosh, speaking of Donnie—I swear, for a guy who hasn't had sex in a while, he sure knows what he's doing. I mean, I had lots of good sex with Liam, but I don't know... I just feel more *adored* with Donnie. The way he touches me and kisses me and makes sure I'm feeling good without making me feel like a delicate flower, it's comforting. I've had guys who would be afraid to toss me around because they think they'll break me, and I mean, I love sensual, passionate sex as much as the next girl, but sometimes I just want to be fucked against the headboard.

"I think we did a great job," I say, high-fiving Donnie after we put the final touches on our sushi rolls. "Can we light it up now?" I wear a naughty grin.

"Should we gather our things in case we need to make a break for it if this goes south?"

"I thought you were confident after watching the YouTube videos again?"

"Well, I am, but remember that time when I asked you to light the grill for me and you almost burned down the apartment complex?"

I gasp and shove his arm. "I did not! The flame went out and… I thought it needed more lighter fluid," I finish with a sheepish smirk as my cheeks turn pink.

He wraps his arm around my shoulder and squeezes me against him. "That flame was huge."

"So are you, but I'm not complaining."

I rub his thigh and tiptoe my fingers flirtatiously towards his cock.

"We have to get through dinner first," he says, laughing and grabbing my hand to stop me from reaching my destination.

"Ugh, fine." I pout my lips.

"You ready?"

I nod, and we take turns lighting our dragon rolls on fire. I watch in amazement as the flame engulfs our sushi roll just like at the restaurant and then slowly fades out.

"Ahh, that was so much fun!" I exclaim as we grab our plates and head for the patio to eat and watch the sunset. I finish my first bite and then ask, "So, do we still have to tell your family that we lied?"

"Yeah, we have to tell them. I don't want the foundation of our relationship to be based off a lie. Don't worry, though, I won't make you be there for it. This was *my* idea, so I'll handle it."

"No, we're a team. We'll face them together." I smile, and so does he.

"Are you sure?"

"Of course I am. You're always there for me; it's my turn to be there for you. I just hope they understand."

"Me too."

Our stomachs are full, our wine glasses have seen two rounds of red wine, and now, we're in our bathing suits, swimming in our infinity pool.

Donnie gets cozy in a corner of the pool, and I swim up next to him, pressing my back against his chest, and he understands the assignment because he immediately wraps me in his warm arms and kisses the top of my head.

"You smell like a coconut," he says, and I turn in his arms and knit my brows, staring up at him. "What? I didn't say it was a bad thing." He smiles, and I roll my eyes with a quirk of my lips, turning back around and leaning into him.

"Thank you for today," I say, staring out towards the dark ocean as the sea breeze tries to sneak between us. "It was perfect."

"Yeah, it was. I'm sorry Olivia surprised us this morning; I know it was kind of awkward."

"No, it's fine. I'll admit, though, I was a little, teeny, tiny bit jealous."

He palms my shoulders and gently spins me around, staring down at me with those beautiful eyes and his pretty smile. They make my heart rate speed up, and the water dripping down his well-built chest doesn't help. I take a deep breath to calm myself, looking at him innocently.

"You were jealous? Why?"

"No, it's stupid. I shouldn't have even said anything. It's not a big deal, anyway."

"If you felt something, it's not stupid. What's up, Kase?"

I sigh and look down at the water, watching the way the water flows around us, like somehow, I'll be able to weasel out of this conversation that I brought on. He lifts my chin back up and stares back at me tenderly.

"I don't know, I just felt kind of insecure, which is weird because I haven't felt like that in so long. But she showed up looking super gorgeous, I was a mess, you were shirtless—and she definitely noticed. I was standing there, and it was like a glance into your past, the way you two looked at each other for a second… Are you sure you want this with me? It's still early—"

"Kasie," his deep voice rumbles, and I swear I love the way he says my name. "I can show you better than I can tell you. So, every day and every night, I will continue to prove to you that you are who I want to be with. You are who I choose. No one but you, okay?"

I nod. "I'm sorry, I know I'm a lot sometimes." I chuckle softly and nervously.

"If you're a lot, I don't want less."

"No matter what?"

"No matter what." He smiles and leans in to seal it with a kiss.

Chapter Twenty

Donnie

~ Day 13, Friday ~

Rehearsal dinner is tonight, but right now, it's time for me—and Kasie—to come clean with my family about our fake-then-not relationship, which is why I've called this afternoon meeting in our room.

Mom, Dad, Mila, and Connor gather around the couch, and each are looking at me curiously, and I wasn't nervous about this until right now.

Kasie interlocks her fingers with mine and gives me an encouraging smile before I begin to address them.

"So, I'm sure you guys are all wondering why I've gathered you here."

"Oh shit, are you pregnant!?" Mila exclaims, looking between Kasie and I.

"What? No! Mila, Kasie's been drinking all vacation long."

"Yeah, and plus I have an IUD," Kasie blurts and then her cheeks flush. "Sorry, probably an overshare."

I shake my head and scoff, trying my best not to laugh. I shove my hand through my hair and then scratch the side of my neck. "Look, guys, I haven't been completely honest with you. Umm, when I told you that Kasie and I were dating, I lied."

And *there* are the looks I was worried about. My mother's disappointment, my father's stern what-the-fuck look, Mila's brows are snapped together, and Connor is scowling like he'd love to give me one of his famous right hooks.

I continue, even though the vibe is awkward as shit right now, "I talked Kasie into it, so please don't be mad at her."

Connor gets up and walks away, ignoring my parents calls for him to stay, as well as mine. He walks out the door and I sigh heavily, moving on.

"Why would you lie?" Mila asks frustratedly.

I'm taller than everyone in this room aside from dad, yet I feel pretty damn low.

"I just wanted to hang out and enjoy this vacation without all the relationship-advice talks. I know it probably doesn't make sense to you guys, but every time I come home for the holidays, Mom, you push and push for me to start dating again. And with Connor and Mila tying the knot, I just knew I'd hear it and get the guilt trip for two weeks. So, I asked Kasie if she would pretend to be my girlfriend so I could have everyone off my back, and I could hang out peacefully."

"Donnie—"

"No, please let me finish because you know what? I've enjoyed my time out here. No one has asked or worried about my relationship status or where my head is at or how I'm living. Everyone did what I knew they would do if I brought Kasie around as my girl. And I didn't even realize how unfair that was to me until a second ago, because I shouldn't feel pressured to date again, like there's some deadline I have to meet. I shouldn't feel like I'm letting you all down because I wanted to enjoy being single.

Mom, I know you were worried about me

after things ended with Olivia, and I gave you every reason to be because I dove straight into partying and started shutting the world out, but I've been better for a while now. Even seeing Olivia yesterday didn't rock me. I'm sorry that I lied, it was selfish. I didn't think everyone would fall for Kasie and me the way they did."

"Uhh, yeah, well you two should take up acting, because you played the part perfectly." Mila looks away, and I can tell the compliment is a sarcastic one.

"Son," my dad says and I'm a little worried that he spoke up before my mom because usually she would have something to say by now. "Do you remember when you were scared to tell me that you didn't want to play pro baseball even though you were offered a full-ride scholarship to Texas Tech to play?"

I scoff. "Yeah, I remember. I thought you'd be pissed."

Dad huffs. "Yet I wasn't. Because you were honest with me. Baseball was *my* dream. Baseball was *Connor's* dream. But it wasn't yours. You didn't want to lose the love of the game, and that was okay. And even though you didn't owe us that explanation, because no one except for you needs to understand the whys in your decisions, you gave it to us because you wanted to be honest and transparent, like you were brought up to be."

I hang my head and sigh. "I know. I let you guys down, and I'm sorry for that."

"Donnie, you didn't let us down." Mom speaks up, and finally I can breathe easy—I think. "We—me, mostly—let *you* down."

"What?" Mila looks flabbergasted, and I bite back my smile because I know she's going to smack me upside my lying-ass head, but I can tell she'll forgive me. I just hope Connor will too, at least before the wedding.

Mom nods. "Yes, I'm disappointed you lied. But I didn't realize what kind of pressure I was putting on you with those conversations. I worry about all my children, and sometimes that worry clouds my judgment. I never meant to make you feel like you had to be dating to make me proud. Donnie, I just want you to be happy. If being single makes you happy, I'm happy too. When my kids are hurting, so am I. I *do* forgive you for lying. Now, can *you* forgive *me* for making you feel down about yourself?"

I walk towards her with these stupid tears in my eyes, and I'm not even really sure why or how they got there. I guess I didn't even realize how much I was holding on to. When she hugs me, I feel like I did when I was a kid who just needed my mom's embrace after skinning my knee.

After the hug, I shake my dad's hand and then look at Mila with apologetic eyes. She rolls her eyes and opens her arms wide for an annoyed hug that I am all too eager to accept.

"Now, go talk to your brother," Mila says, giving me the smack to my head like I knew she would.

I start towards the door and the spin back around. "Oh, and one more thing. As of the bachelor party night, Kasie and I are officially dating…for real this time." I hurry out the door as I hear excited gasps and questions being tossed at Kasie from all sides—hopefully she won't be to upset that I threw that out and darted.

When the door shuts behind me, I expect to have to look for Connor, but he's sitting against the wall in the hallway.

"Please tell me you heard that," I ask,

hoping I can get away without having to explain to him too, and also hoping that he heard my mom's forgiveness, which in turn, would make it easier for him to offer his.

"Most of it," he mutters, and I realize I'm not getting away so easily. "I'm your brother, man. Growing up, you used to tell me everything. Shit, you even told me about your stupid plan to throw that big-ass party when mom and dad took me out of town to see the Tigers play the Yankees in New York."

I scoff, sitting down beside him. "I was sixteen, with the house to myself all weekend. I wasn't going to *not* throw a party. I just never expected it to turn into the biggest party of the year."

He laughs gently, almost like he didn't want to but couldn't help himself.

I'm getting somewhere.

"I don't blame you; I would have done the same. But even sixteen-year-old Donnie knew he could tell his brother anything and it would stay between them. I feel like I don't even know you anymore, bro. We used to be so close. Now, we barely talk, and you're halfway across the country, living life, which is awesome, but I miss you, man. Visiting twice a year for a couple days on Thanksgiving and Christmas, it just doesn't feel like it should be like that. And this year, I only saw and talked to you more because of my wedding, but what happens after this?"

"You know you're always welcome to visit me *too*, right? I mean, I love coming home for the holidays, and truth be told, I could probably come around more often, but you've never mentioned anything about coming to see me and my place and all that shit."

"No, you're right. It's on me, too… We need to do better, though. The last thing I want is to go through life and realize the days, months, and years are passing us by and we barely know or speak to one another. I don't mean to throw all this on you like this, it's just, when coach passed away last year, it made me realize that life is fucking short. He lived a good, long-ass life, but what if it was me or you who was gone unexpectedly? I don't want to live with wishing I had done things differently."

"Yeah, I get it, bro. Damn, I didn't even

know you were struggling."

"We're guys. Conversations like this don't happen until they do. It shouldn't be that way, though. Let's make a vow right now; if one of us is struggling, we got to speak up. To each other, to our ladies, to someone. But you need to know I always got your back, so you can always talk to me."

"Same, I've got you brother. I love you, man."

"I love you, too."

He sticks his hand out, and I grip it for a handshake and a hug. And then he slugs me in the arm.

"Damn, bro. How does your old ass still have all that power behind your punch?" I whine, wincing and rubbing my arm as he chuckles with a shit-eating grin.

"Lie to me again and it'll be your face, little bro."

While the day may have started out awkward with Kasie and I confessing to our sham relationship and then immediately after that pulling a cheesy-ass infomercial "But wait, there's more!" by actually really dating—I'm happy that it turned into a pretty awesome day. My family still loves her, and the wedding rehearsal went off without a hitch—Mila's smile was brighter than the sun that was shining down on all of us. And the rehearsal dinner at the waterfront steakhouse was entertaining, thanks to Nate and Marcus getting so drunk that after dinner, they went to the balcony behind the restaurant, stripped down to their underwear, and jumped the guardrail into the ocean. And Connor, Gavin, and I had to join them to make sure their drunk asses didn't drown—Lavelle never learned how to swim and has no intention of it, so he was lucky enough to stay topside. Although, it was kind of therapeutic, once my body warmed up.

But now that all the festivities are done—and I've showered and changed into a pair of jeans and a T-shirt—Kasie and I are walking hand in hand along the beach. The moon is extra bright tonight, bringing out the sparkle in her pretty eyes, and the ocean waves are the perfect background noise for our conversation.

"Aside from you stripping and soaking those sexy muscles in the ocean tonight, it was fun hearing stories about you and Connor's childhood shenanigans," she says and then grins. "I especially liked your dad's *initiative* story."

I scoff and side-eye her, which makes her laugh and look away while tucking strands of her hair behind her ear.

There you go stealing my heart again.

I'm just glad that now I can embrace these feelings when they race through my body. It still doesn't feel real sometimes, that she's mine. I swear I've never wanted anything as much as I want us to stay together. I'm still scared of what happens if things don't work out between us, but at the same time, I can't think about what if, so I'm confident that the path I'm on is the right one.

"You know, I don't think he will ever let me live that down. I knew I was right for being suspicious when, instead of sending Connor to the automotive store since he knows everything about cars, he sent me to get the can of initiative, when I know just enough about cars to get by. I was searching for a good twenty minutes before I gave up and asked someone…and quickly wished I hadn't. He really did the most just to get me off my ass to help him with some yardwork when he could have just asked."

"Yeah, but where's the fun in that?" she asks, and then pats my arm like she's trying to console me, but she's not. "It's okay, though, you definitely know how to take initiative *now*." She winks and wiggles her brows as she nods at my crotch.

A lopsided grin splits my face, and she bites the corner of her bottom lip, looking at me with those moonlit eyes.

"Kasie Pearce, are you flirting with me?"

"Nope, not one bit. I'm innocent," she says, trying to look as pure and virginal as possible.

"Come here." I pull her into my arms, and she lets out a spirited scream as I cover her with kisses.

After the last kiss leaves my lips, we stare at each other under the stars, silent, but our eyes are saying everything that needs to be said. And that's probably a good thing, because my heart is beating so fast that even if I tried to talk right now, I'd just be catching my breath.

Whatever's between us, it doesn't fade when we get back to our room. And while she's riding me, I'm not just watching the pleasure on her face or listening to it in her moans, I'm admiring this strong, beautiful girl who, in all her delicate ways, was able to make me believe in love again. It's crazy to even say that, because while I love her as a best friend, and I'm not *in* love with her romantically just yet, but I can admit that I can see myself loving her.

She looks down at me with that heart-stopping smile as she grinds her hips. I can feel her temperature rising as she increases the speed and bites her lips to try—unsuccessfully—to stop herself from being too loud.

I flip her to her back and suck on her nipples as I push inside of her, and then raise one of her legs in the air as I raise up too. I thrust slow and deep in her warm, wet pussy for a while before lowering her leg back down and flipping her to her side as I position myself behind her. I wrap her in my arms and move her long, blonde hair out of the way of her neck. I'm kissing and caressing her, hoping that she can feel just how much I need her; there's no one in this world I'd ever leave her for. Even when she drives me crazy, she won't ever drive me away.

Kasie nestles her head back into me as I continue to softly kiss and bite her neck. And then she gasps quietly when I slide my hard cock back inside of her. I run my hand down her sternum to her stomach and then to her clit, playing with it while I'm steadily thrusting in and out. I increase the speed of my fingers and thrusts, and that increases the volume and frequency of her raspy breaths. I feel her pussy getting wetter as her lips drag up and down my cock, until I pull out, pin her on her back, and push inside of her again.

"Don't stop," she rasps, squirming beneath me, her breath shallow and quick. "Harder," she begs, and I listen. "Harder!" she screams again, digging her nails into my skin and arching her back while I pound her until her eyes roll back.

Kasie's moaning, I'm grunting, and just a moment later, we come together, an internal explosion so intense I nearly black out before dropping down beside her.

Chapter Twenty One

Kasie

~ Day 14, Saturday ~

My pussy is still pulsing and tingling from the pleasure Donnie just dished out. I'm all sweaty from hot sex, and my hair is a mess, yet somehow, I still feel as beautiful as I will in a bit when I'm all dolled up for the wedding. Maybe it's the way Donnie can't keep his eyes—and hands—off me even after we've had sex, or maybe it's the way he pulled me into his arms right after we finished, or it could even be the barrage of little kisses to my temple that I just received from him. Whatever it is, I don't care, I just know I'm soaking it all in and hoping this honeymoon stage doesn't come to a halt when we're no longer in paradise and surrounded by an aura of love.

When our breakfast and cherry mimosas arrive, Donnie and I get set up outside on our bedroom patio. The sun is covered by some clouds from last night's rain, but the clouds and sky are still bright, so it's nice that we'll still have a sunshiney day.

"How's your cinnamon roll?" Donnie asks as I lift an icing-filled cinnamon roll bite to my mouth. "Is it as good as the ones you make?"

"It's prettier," I say after swallowing the delicious bite.

He waves his hands to dismiss my humble comment. "You can work on presentation; what's most important is that everything you make is fucking flavorful and delicious."

"You're sure about that? You wouldn't lie to me just to stay out of the dugout?"

"The dugout?"

I look at him like he's crazy, because *he's* the baseball player here. How does he not know what I'm referring to?

"Yes, the dugout. You know, where you go when you get in trouble on the field."

He cracks up laughing, and I narrow my eyes at him. "You don't go to the dugout when you get in trouble."

I tilt my head with confusion. "Wait, then, where do you go? It sounds like it should be a place of punishment."

"I mean, the worst that can happen is you get ejected from the game. I think you're talking about the penalty box, but that's for hockey."

Either I'm blushing or the bright sun shining on my face just got warmer. "Ohhhh."

He smiles affectionately "Anyways, no, I wouldn't lie to you, Kase. You are an extremely talented baker who, admittedly, is still learning how to make things look as pretty as you, but you'll get there."

"Aww, you are so sweet. Okay, good, I just wanted to make sure because when Olivia and I were talking the other night, she told me this story about you eating her pie—"

"Like, *actual* pie, right?"

"Oh my gosh, yes, *actual* pie." I chuckle, shaking my head. "Get your mind out of the gutter. Moving on. She told me about the time she wanted to surprise you with your favorite apple pie and it was a total fail, yet you ate it up like that lattice crust was not thick and doughy. I thought it was sweet, but I also want to make sure that you tell me if what I make isn't good, so I can improve. Deal?" I offer my hand.

"You won't get mad?" He looks at me like he doesn't trust this deal.

"Well, I mean, obviously say it nicely, but no, I won't get mad if it's constructive."

"Hold on, let me record this for proof, just in case."

"Ugh, Donnie." I give him a look that says he's got half a second to shake my hand before he's going to spend some time in the penalty box—*not* the dugout.

He laughs, grabbing my outstretched hand, and for a moment I almost forget why because I'm lost in the sound of his laugh. I love the way he laughs. He sounds so alive and happy.

"All right, you've got a deal, Miss Pearce," he says, his tone deep and sexy, before letting my hand go.

I lick my lips. "Oh, I like the sound of that.

It makes me feel like I'm your sexy boss or something."

He grazes his leg against mine from under the table. "Do you want to be? Tell me what you want me to do to you, and I'll do it."

I press my index finger to my lip and look up out of the corner of my eyes like I'm thinking. "Hmm… Do you *really* want to know what I want you to do to me?"

"Yeah," he says, lowering his eyes and voice, trying to be sexy, so I give him a flirty gaze.

"Do my makeup, so I can just sit there and sip wine like a queen today."

He throws his hands in the air and rolls his eyes with a frustrated grunt, which makes me crack up with laughter. "That is *not* what I expected."

"You know what else I bet you didn't expect?"

"What's that?" he asks before shoveling another bite in his mouth.

"I can tie a knot in a cherry stem with my tongue."

He finishes his bite, looking at me suspiciously. "That's impossible."

"What? No, it isn't. I can do it. I swear."

"Ok, then show me. If you can do it, I'll let you have the rest of my fruits."

"How much pineapple is in there?" I ask, trying to inspect his fruit bowl from my end of the table. He picks his fruit bowl up and tilts it, so I can see there are plenty of pineapple chunks—my favorite. "All right, you've got a deal. Give me the cherry out of your mimosa."

He laughs. "Nope, you can only use yours. You get one chance at it."

"Ugh, fine. I haven't done it since like high school. I used to practice it religiously, trying to prove I was a good kisser. I'm pretty sure my dad wondered where my sudden taste for cherries came from." I giggle. I take the cherry out of my mimosa and remove the stem, flirtatiously putting it in my mouth, and the intrigue on Donnie's face makes it worth it. I start working my tongue, trying to remember how I used to do it.

He's watching me like a hawk, with this confident look on his face, like he just *knows* I'm going to fail, but when I'm sure I got the knot in the stem, I squeal with happiness and take it out of my mouth, showing it to him like it's a trophy.

He widens his eyes and drops his jaw, and I'm pretty sure there's a glimmer of pride in his eyes. "All right, you know what? I'm not even mad. That's sexy."

I smile proudly. "Thank you. Now hand over your fruit, loser." He does, and I happily pick out the pineapple chunks and choose which one I'm going to save for last, because I always save the best bite for last. I pop one in my mouth and look up, noticing he's staring at me endearingly. "What?" I tuck my hair behind my ear, feeling oddly bashful because I don't usually feel this way in his presence.

"You're just so pretty when you smile."

And with that, I can't stop my smile from growing, even if I tried. In fact, I'm probably smiling like Harley Quinn right now.

"You make it easy to."

He pushes his chair out and leans his tall ass over the table to kiss me.

I love these kisses. I don't ever want to get used to this.

He sits back in his seat and grabs his cherry mimosa to take a sip before looking at me with an amused smirk. "You're not going to start calling me sweet cheeks or honey muffin or some other random nickname now, are you?"

I laugh and narrow my eyes at him. "Umm, I wasn't going to, but honey muffin sounds cute, I think I'll go with that," I say, letting him stew in the disappointment a little before continuing, "I'm kidding. I was totally onboard with the cute nicknames for our fake relationship, but I've called you Donnie, loser, and weirdo for so long that I don't think I could really call you baby or honey. It feels kind of weird."

"Yeah, it does." He pauses and then asks, "But kissing, having sex, and doing all these other affectionate things isn't awkward for you, is it?"

"Oh, no, not at all. I *did* think there would be this awkward phase where we would have to get used to it, but maybe our little trial period of dating helped to ease that or something." I giggle, toying with a lock of hair. "Is it awkward for you?"

"Nope," he says, shaking his head. "I'm just glad I don't have to hide being hard around you anymore because *that* was awkward."

I widen my eyes. "Wait, what? When did this happen?"

He bursts into laughter, almost knocking his drink off the table. "Our first kiss."

"In the ocean? I guess that makes sense. That was pretty hot."

"No… I mean, yes, I was hard then too but I'm talking about our first, first kiss."

"Ohhhh… Hold on, is that why you ran off, worried about your missing wallet?" I ask, and he cracks a grin. I drop my jaw and point my index finger accusingly at his chest. "I knew something was off!"

"It's not *my* fault. Maybe if you hadn't practiced tying knots in cherry stems with your tongue, you wouldn't be such an amazing kisser."

I scrunch up my nose with a teasing glare as I cut another piece of my cinnamon roll and then stuff it into my mouth.

Chapter Twenty Two

Donnie

After no one objects, the vows are exchanged, and the kiss to seal the marriage is witnessed, the reception is in full swing. Smiles are at every flower-decorated table as Connor and Mila take Hennessey shots at each one—although, some of us guys and girls in the wedding party tag in to take some of the shots for the bride and groom so they don't end up face-down on the dance floor. Penelope and I knock our speeches out of the park, we eat the delicious food that the resort provided, as well as the home-cooked food that Mila's mom made, which was fucking bomb! And now, Kasie and I are in the middle of the packed dance floor, dancing to a slow song.

"They're so cute," Kasie says, looking over at Connor and Mila slow dancing together. "It was super sweet when Connor started tearing up as she was walking down the aisle. I was totally crying too. I had to go fix my makeup as soon as the ceremony was over."

"It *was* pretty sweet, but I'm a little salty that he didn't save any tears for my speech."

"Aww, your speech was good, baby," she says, and we both pause, looking at each other, probably both analyzing how awkward that just felt. "Yeah, no, that's not happening yet. I wanted to try saying it out loud to see if I could do it, but yeah, it's definitely weird." We both laugh and then she continues. "Anyway, at least your speech had everyone rolling with laughter, especially Connor."

"Yeah, that's true. All right, he's forgiven."

"Can I cut in?" a familiar voice asks, and I don't have to turn my head to know it's Olivia.

She's standing there wearing a blue dress and a gentle smile, waiting for Kasie's approval.

"Yeah, of course," Kasie says. "I'll go get us some drinks." She leans up, and I meet her halfway for a kiss.

"Is everything okay?" I ask, looking into Olivia's eyes as I take her hand and we sway back and forth.

I make sure to put enough distance in between us that it's clear this dance is between two friends. Especially after Kasie's admission of feeling a bit insecure the other day, I want to make sure if she's watching—which I imagine she is because *I* would be—she knows I'm taking our new relationship seriously.

"Yeah," she says, breaking eye contact for a second and then looking back up at me. She clears her throat. "I just wanted to make sure I had a chance to say goodbye."

"You're leaving tonight?"

She nods. "I've got a test to study for all day tomorrow, so I've got a redeye to catch in a couple hours."

"Well, good luck…with your future and stuff."

"Thanks." She tucks a curl behind her ear and smiles a dimpled smile. "I think I'm going to go to New York, after I finish my nursing program."

"Really? That's big, Olivia!"

"Yeah, I've always wanted to go."

"I remember."

"I have your girlfriend to thank. She reminded me the other night that there's no growth in your comfort zone...and I've been comfortable all my life." She takes a deep breath. "But it's time for a change. I'm scared but—"

"You'll be all right. You'll kill it in New York."

"Thank you. When I get settled, maybe one day I could take you and Kasie around, show you the sights."

I nod, we hug, and she lets go of my hand, starting to walk away. I call after her, "Hey, Olivia."

She turns around with a soft look in her eyes. "Yes, Donnie?"

"I'm glad you came."

Her smile widens. "Me, too."

Good luck, Olivia. I truly want the best for you.

~ Day 15, Sunday ~

"I can't believe it's over," Kasie says, leaning back into my embrace as we watch our last sunrise together at Enchanted Shores.

I kiss the top of her head, holding her close and taking everything this moment is giving, from Kasie's floral scent from her perfume, the way I can feel her relaxed breaths almost mirroring mine while I'm holding her against my chest, to the wind playing with her hair. The memories from this trip are replaying in the back of my head, memories that will always make this place extra special for me— and hopefully for her too. It's the place where my heart started to beat again. The place where my best friend gave me my heart back and then stole it all over again when she became my girl. This place, it's *our* place.

"We'll come back."

Chapter Twenty Three

Kasie

Ten months later…

Dirty measuring cups and spoons are spread across the counter, my apron has a new vanilla stain, the oven is screaming that the second batch of chocolate chip cookies are done, and I'm flustered because I can't remember where I set the Ziploc bags—somewhere within this mess, clearly. I open the oven and am about grab the cookie sheet without an oven mitt, but thankfully, as soon as I feel the heat radiating from it, it clicks in my busy mind, and I grab the oven mitt to bring the cookies out and set them on top of the oven.

I know I'm just feeling overwhelmed right now because Donnie and I were supposed to be traveling back to my hometown tomorrow to visit my dad, which I was excited about until Donnie's stupid boss picked up some rich client in Beverly

Hills who wants to go over a project—and naturally, the world will end if it's not this weekend. So, now, not only will I be getting on a plane *by myself* for the first time since I moved to California, but if—and I use that word lightly because I'm certain it will happen—I run into my ex, I'll be alone.

I hate that after all these years, the thought of seeing him still sends me into a spin of anxiety and worrisome thoughts. But according to my therapist, I've got some unhealed trauma from being the star of a video that was taken without my consent. Which is why, sometimes, loud restaurants and groups of people laughing uncontrollably make me uncomfortable, sending me into panic mode. After she helped me unpack that, Donnie and I decided that I need to take back control and go back to my hometown to let go of my trauma.

"There they are," I mutter to myself when I find the Ziploc bags.

I grab them and then a cookie from the first batch that's cooled down now. First, I bite into the warm, chewy chocolate chip cookie to taste it, and my mom's recipe wins again.

These cookies have always been my favorite

to make, ever since I was a little girl. They're easy, yummy, and always come out chewy in the middle and crunchy around the edges.

I wipe the chocolate from the corner of my mouth and start piling the cookies into one of the Ziploc bags for Donnie to take with him on his road trip. He'll probably have all these eaten before he gets there.

I hear him rolling his suitcase from the hallway, and a second later, he appears, dressed in ripped blue jeans, a white T-shirt, and a baseball cap.

Gosh, he looks so sexy.

And me? Well, my apron is dirty, my forearm is sticky from leaning on the counter earlier where I spilled some sugar, I don't have any makeup on, and my hair's up in a messy bun. Oh, and I'm pretty sure I didn't get all the chocolate off my mouth.

He takes one look at me and smiles this sweet smile that comforts me and somehow makes me feel like I'm all dressed up and about to go out with my girls. As comforted as I am, I'm also starting to feel like my breaths are racing each other.

Donnie rolls his suitcase to the front door and then starts my way.

He stops halfway and sneezes. "Bless you, baby," I say.

"I am as long as you're here." He smirks, and my body temperature rises.

"Aww." I giggle affectionately. "Come here, my sweet and cheesy man." I cup his stubbled chin and bring his lips in for a kiss when he's in front of me.

"Are these for me?" He asks, grabbing the bag full of cookies.

"Mm-hm." I smile gently, trying not to show him that I'm feeling anxious along with trying not to let this anxiety turn into a panic attack, but I should know by now that I can't ignore it.

And I should also know that he knows me all too well, because he palms my shoulders and looks me in the eyes when he says, "Hey, you've got this. You don't need me to be there; you're strong enough on your own."

I take a deep breath in through my nose, hold it for four seconds, and then breathe out completely, and thankfully it's calming enough to be helpful right now.

"I can't believe I'm doing this."

"I can. You're capable of anything you set your mind to. And trust me, it's time for you to go back home and leave your past in the past. That's the whole point of this trip, remember?" He kisses my pouty lips and then says, "When you get back, we'll celebrate. We'll grab a box of wine, you can fill our glasses too full like you always do, and we'll even discuss you officially moving in with me."

"Really?" I say, my eyes lighting up at the idea of moving in together, and suddenly the gloom I'm feeling melts away a little. "Did you finally pick up my subtle hint from the other night?"

He creases his brows and looks at me like I'm crazy. "That was your idea of a subtle hint? Telling me how sad you are that I won't be able to surprise you with a key to my place because you've already had one for forever?"

I give him a side-eye and say, "Okay, fine, I

know I don't do subtle, but you didn't even say anything when I hinted at it."

He brings me closer and my body tingles. His deep voice caresses my eardrums. "I'm saying something now."

"Not just to make me worry less about the trip though, right? Because I don't want you to force us moving in together if you're not ready. I can wait. Like we said when we got back from your brother's wedding, we don't have to rush anything."

"No, I'm ready, Kasie. Having you stay the night over here every other weekend has only made me want you here more. It feels like the right time to take the next step in our relationship."

I smile and breathe calmly. "I agree. Well, you should probably get going or you'll be late."

I hug him tight and feel his warm arms wrap around me, holding me against his chest like we're going to be apart for longer than just a few days.

After what seems like an hour in each other's arms, I let go and back away, giving him an encouraging shove or he'll never get out of here. He's always running late anyway, but when I'm here, he's usually later than he already is because we can't keep our hands off each other—which I love. "Okay, you should go before I start tearing up." I choke laugh, using my index finger to wipe the corner of my eyes where they're getting wet.

I'm not even on my period! Why am I so emotional right now? Reel it in, Kasie. You would think this was goodbye or something.

A smile forms on his face as he brings me in for a quick kiss. "I love you."

I sigh happily to myself. I swear, I will never tire of hearing those words leave his lips.

"I love you too."

The next day…

The flight into South Carolina was smooth and easy. I text Donnie to let him know I miss him and that I landed safely. He texts me back pretty quickly, letting me know he misses me too and that he'll be able to call me soon. I put my phone away, grab my luggage from the carousel, and find my dad shortly after.

When we get to his car, it's like nothing has changed. It's still the same rusty orange color, it's still got the same dent in the back bumper where I backed into a light pole in the school parking lot, and it still acts like it's not going to start but does. The rush of familiarity eases my mind a little.

We start the thirty-minute journey from the airport to our hometown, and my dad tells me to look in the center console.

I open it up and squeal with happiness. "Is this for me?" I ask, grabbing the bag full of my favorite chocolate fudge from a little shop in town. He nods and I hurry a piece out. "Ahh, Daddy, you're the best!" I exclaim before biting into the fudge. "Thank you."

He just smiles and looks over at me with tears in his eyes—happy tears, maybe? I don't know, it doesn't seem like a happy-tear worthy moment. I mean, it's just fudge.

I look at him curiously, finishing my bite before asking, "Is everything okay?"

He takes a deep breath, focusing back on the road. "I'm just happy to have you back home after all these years."

It seems like there's more, but if there is, he doesn't say it. I sit back in my seat and take a picture of the fudge, sending it to Donnie and promising him I'll save him some—that or I'll have to run out to the store and get more for him before heading back home, if I should happen to eat it all, which is a pretty distinct possibility.

My dad pulls into the familiar driveway, we walk inside, and all the fond memories of being here flood my mind. Like the car, everything here still looks like it did when I left. I kick my boots off and put the milk in the fridge. "So, should we throw on some Bulls re-runs and pop some popcorn for old time's sake? We've got an hour and half before we have to be at our dinner reservation."

My dad laughs and says, "That sounds like a great idea, sweet pea. But first, can you run out to the back patio to grab my bottle opener? The weather was beautiful last night, and I forgot to bring it in."

"Sure," I say, starting for the door.

"You didn't want to put your boots back on?"

I giggle and look at him askance, because why would I?

"I know I'm a city girl now, Daddy, but I'm still a southern girl at heart. I can go barefoot."

"Okay, okay, suit yourself."

I shake my head, laughing to myself as I open the back door and step outside.

As soon as I do, I hear "Marry Me" by Train start to play, and a bunch of shushes. I see Morgan and Mila and Connor and Donnie's family, and our friends, all gathered in my dad's backyard, looking up at me with smiles. I hear sniffles, and that's when it hits me.

I turn around and my dad is standing there, smiling, with tears in his eyes, and now they're in mine too.

"Oh my gosh!" I cover a gasp with my hands and look at him as if to ask if this is really happening.

He answers with a nod, and I look over the

balcony, and my heart fills with so much love that I feel almost too full to breathe. I see Donnie, smiling at me like he's never done before. He's standing in the middle of a heart made of red rose petals right there in the lush green grass. He's dressed in dress pants, a button-up, and a tie—I can see now why my dad was adamant that I be dressed and ready for dinner before I got here. Thank goodness I listened and paired my knee-high boots with my long-sleeved, form-fitting dress.

I start walking down the stairs and I run to Donnie, throwing my arms around him, and just soaking in this moment. Everything is perfect. The sun is shining, the breeze makes the warm weather just cool enough to be comfortable, the sky is the cutest shade of baby blue, and the trees are blooming and colorful.

"I thought you were... how did you... I'm so confused." I choke laugh as tears slide down my cheeks. I don't even care if my makeup is messed up right now.

"There was no rich client in Beverly Hills," he says, chuckling. "There was no work trip, only this trip. I've been planning this with your dad for a couple months now. Getting you onboard to come out here, convincing you to let me book the trip so you don't see that I booked our flights a day apart— that was the hardest part, by the way." He laughs, and so does everyone around us, because I think they all know by now that I like having control.

He takes my hand in his and looks at me with his pretty green eyes. He clears his throat as his eyes start to water, which doesn't help mine to dry up. "Kasie, you once told me that one day some girl was going to come along and make me believe in love again. I laughed it off, but little did I know that girl would be you. Over the past ten months that we've been together, I've come to realize that the beautiful moments of my life aren't just *with* you, they're *because* of you. Seeing you smile, hearing you laugh, feeling your love in every embrace and every kiss, it makes me feel so lucky that I get to share my life with you. And even though forever will never be long enough, I want to spend it with you by my side.

So, Kasie Pearce…" He pauses and wipes his eyes, taking a deep breath as he lowers himself to one knee. He reaches in his pocket, and I swear everything is in slow-mo right now except for my racing heart. I've never felt so happy and excited and hopeful and just everything good as I do in this moment. He opens the box, showing me the most beautiful diamond ring that I've ever seen, and asks, "Will you spend forever with me?"

Tears stream down my cheek as I exclaim, "Yes!"

He slips the ring on my finger, stands to his feet, and caresses my cheek as we share a steamy first kiss as betrotheds. When our lips part, I just stare into his eyes, lost in the moment with the man I'm going to marry. The cheers and clapping all around us seem like they're in the distance.

"I love you," he whispers with a smile.

"I love you too...with my whole heart, for my whole life."

The next day...

After all the excitement and celebrating with all our favorite people yesterday, Donnie, my dad, and I get ready and head into town in the early afternoon to show Donnie around. I take him to all my favorite places, and save the best for last, Loretta's Fudge Shoppe. When we walk in, Miss Loretta is finishing up with a customer. When she sees me, she squeals with happiness as she hurries around the counter to wrap me in a big, grandma-type hug.

I introduce her to Donnie and fill her in on all the highlights since I've been gone, especially my new fiancée status! I can't believe I get to say that now. Ahhh, my heart is so happy. His proposal was everything I ever wanted. I'm still surprised he and my dad were able to pull it off without me knowing.

Loretta and I get to talking more, and Donnie and my dad let us know they'll be across the street at the car show.

Being back home, it's nice. I feel liberated and at peace, being here. I also feel in control, like I'm taking back what's mine.

"Well, you be sure to let me know when your bakery is open for business," Loretta tells me as we finish our conversation. "Mel and I will make a special trip just for you. I am so proud of you, young lady, as would your mother be."

"Thank you so much. I wish that she could be there to see when I open it, but I know she's up in heaven smiling down."

"She most certainly is."

Several customers come in and Loretta bids me farewell as she goes to help them. I get ready to leave so I can join my dad and Donnie at the car show, when my ex, Greg, walks in on a mission.

He's as tall as I remember, and even though his muscles aren't as defined as they once were, he still has his linebacker size. His jet-black hair is shoulder-length now instead of buzzed, and his clean-shaven face is replaced with a scruffy beard.

"I thought I'd find you here," he says, his voice gruff and almost accusing, like I was supposed to tell him I was coming or something.

"Well, I wasn't looking for *you*, so congratulations?"

My heart is beating so fast right now, but I feel in control. I don't feel scared or intimidated like I thought I would.

"Oh, come on. Do you *really* still hate me?"

"What do you want, Greg? Clearly, you want something, or you wouldn't have searched me out like a creeper."

"Damn, California changed you. You look the same, but fuck, you've got a little more sass now. It's kind of sexy. You know, if you weren't such a pushover back then, maybe we'd still be together. Hell, we may even be married."

I laugh hysterically. "Do you see that guy across the street, standing with my dad?" Greg turns his head to look. "That's the kind of man worth marrying. A man who makes me feel protected and strong at the same time. A man who loves me unconditionally, even through all my insecurities and struggles. That man right there is my fiancé, and if it wasn't for you being the piece of shit that you are, I may never have found him. So, thank you, Greg. Thank you for being a piece of shit, so that I could push myself to become the best version of me. And with that, I hope I never see you again. And if I do, feel free not to talk to me."

He huffs as I begin walking confidently towards the door. I nearly shoulder bump him, but he moves slightly before I do.

I walk out the door and hear him mutter something, but I ignore him and leave him the past where he belongs. I take a deep, calming, accomplished breath, smiling to myself as I walk to meet up with my dad and my fiancé.

I'm finally free.

Epilogue

Donnie

Two years later...

I toss the empty box in the back of the storage room. "All right, I think we're officially ready," I holler loud enough for Kasie to hear from the cash register. I turn around to go join her, so we can head outside where everyone else is gathered. "Oh shit!" I exclaim, startled. "I thought you were at the register," I say to Kasie, who's standing against the doorway of the storage room with an inviting look in her eyes.

We've been so busy prepping all morning that I've barely had a chance to just look at her, but now that I've got some time to admire my sexy wife, I look her up and down. Her long, blonde hair falls perfectly over her shoulders. Her tied-up white T-shirt shows just a peek at her toned stomach. And her short skirt shows off her flawless, sun-kissed legs.

Damn, you're looking so good.

She doesn't say a word. She just smiles a flirty smile, shuts the storage room door, and catwalks across the room until she and the soft, floral scent from her perfume are occupying my bubble space, which I'm more than happy to share with her.

"I'm so wet right now," Kasie whispers in my ear, rubbing her hand against my cock from the outside of my jeans.

"Baby, your ribbon cutting ceremony starts in ten minutes," I say, but it doesn't deter her. It just seems to excite her even more.

"We've got time for a quickie," she says with a twinkle in her eyes.

She wraps her hand around the back of my head and brings my lips down to hers, kissing me wildly. We stumble backward, knocking something off the table that clangs onto the ground.

"Do we though?" I ask in between hungry kisses to my lips and neck.

"I want you inside me," she begs, ignoring my question. She unbuttons my jeans and slides her hand inside my boxers to grab my hardening cock. Her eyes widen. "We can make time. It's our tradition. We had sex the first day we got together in Punta Cana, the first day we moved in together, the first day of our marriage at the Chateau de Carsix, and now we have to on the first day my bakery will be open. I don't make the rules, I just follow them."

"*You* following rules? Riiight," I scoff and then reach my hand under her skirt to feel just how wet she is.

She wears a sexy smirk, and in one motion, I grab her shoulders to spin her around, which makes her gasp excitedly. I pull my cock out, hike up her skirt, slide her panties to the side, and push into her.

"Oh my gosh." She moans as I begin thrusting into her, pressing her against the storage wall. I can feel her gripping my cock and, fuck, she feels so good.

I slide my hand inside her shirt, running my hand from her stomach to her boobs. I slip my hand inside her bra and twist her nipples, still thrusting the moans from her lips until they're in unison with my grunts.

This right here is what I adore about our life together. It's full of closeness, spontaneity, love, and just a general overall affection for each other. Growing up, I always imagined living a life like this, but I don't think I ever truly believed it would happen. But this girl right here, the girl who I can't get enough of, she's my dream come true.

A minute later—and just in time because we're running out of it—she comes in between pleasured screams and I tumble after her a moment later.

She pulls her skirt back down and smooths it.

"I'm going to run to the bathroom to fix my hair and touch-up my lipstick that you messed up," she says with a devious smile, and I pinch her ass as she walks away.

When she comes back out, we interlock our fingers and start walking toward the front door of her bakery. The red ribbon is there, the people are lined up, our friends are in the front of the crowd, and it's a beautiful sight to see.

She stops when we get halfway to the door, and peers around the bakery.

"Are you okay?" I ask.

She nods. "I just want to take a second and soak this all in. I can't believe this is finally happening." She smiles and sighs happily.

"I'm proud of you, sweetheart."

I hug her and give her a kiss before we walk out to the ribbon-cutting ceremony to celebrate the first official day of our new adventure together. Another adventure that we get to write in *our* adventure journal.

About the Author

Hey! I'm Emory Grey! I'm just your typical indie romance author writing happily after evers. But when I'm not, I'm creating my own happily ever after with my little family, enjoying the little things in life and doing my best not to take anything for granted. Being an author is my dream but being a loyal husband and loving father is what I love most about my life!

Connect with Emory Grey:

Instagram:
https://instagram.com/emorygreyauthor

Facebook:
https://www.facebook.com/emorygreyauthor/

Goodreads:
https://www.goodreads.com/user/show/146721494

TikTok:
www.tiktok.com/@emorygreyauthor

59233789R00219